HIS DAUGHTER'S BEST FRIEND

NATASHA L. BLACK

INTRODUCTION

**I need this internship to help pay for law school
I'm lucky my friend convinced her dad to
hire me.**

He's intimidating, sexy and grouchy as hell that he agreed to
help out some sorority girl.
We try to resist, but our chemistry is just too much.
Con and I spend a scorching night together.

My bestie can never know I've fallen into bed with her dad,
That I've fallen in love with him.

His vindictive ex tells his daughter about us.
My bff hates me. Con and I can never be together now.
I leave LA for good, go back to my small hometown,
With a broken heart and a huge secret.
Once so sure about my future, now I have no idea what I'm
going to do.

**One morning I come down to breakfast to find
him sitting at my mom's table,
Might I actually get my happily ever after?**

1

CON

Pictures of beautiful women covered my desk. I shuffled through them, sorting them into *yes* and *no* piles. I didn't have a *maybe* category. Either they fit the look the producer was looking for, or they didn't. I rolled my shoulders back, trying to dislodge the creeping sensation that I wasn't going to find the *one* in here. Irritation prickled behind my eyes as the flawless, symmetrical, dark-eyed women began to run together. Normally, I wasn't getting my hands dirty with mid-levels and unknowns like this, but the producer was Julian Lewis, one of my closest friends.

"It's like Tinder," our mutual friend Garrett observed, lounging back in one of my conference chairs. "Except you actually still print shit out." He had one ankle crossed over his knee, and he was alternating between tossing one of my autographed baseballs in the air and scrolling through his phone.

"I'm old school," I muttered, unoffended. I skidded the last picture to the *no* side and stared at the empty gulf between the piles like a new one might appear if I gave it a minute. A whole new stack would appear within minutes if I told my assistant to make it happen. There was never a shortage of headshots. Hundreds of them came into the mailroom every day, unsolicited. The problem was me. I needed a break.

"Finally," Garrett said when he saw me push back from my desk. He slapped the ball back in its holder and stood up. "Let's go. I need a drink."

I took another minute to straighten each pile and then adjust the baseball in its holder so that the blue-scrawled *Sandy Koufax* signature, sandwiched between the red stitching, was facing out. Garrett, who had headed out without checking to make sure I was behind him, came back and knocked impatiently on the glass wall between my office and the hallway.

I held up a finger and pushed in the chairs around the conference table, including the one Garrett had left pulled out and spun around to face the window. Then, just to piss him off, I watered the plants I had around my office.

When I finally joined him in the hall, he looked exasperated. "You literally pay someone to do that shit for you."

I gave him the finger and didn't bother answering. Garrett probably had included cleaning up after him in his EA's job profile. I hadn't. It wouldn't have been worth it. I knew I was anal retentive about my space and my plants, and it was easier to do it myself than to train someone. Besides, my executive assistant Maureen she kept my life running and was a good friend . She'd laugh in my face if I asked her to clean up after me considering how much work she did already.

"We did it," Garrett said when we made it to the street. "Another fucking week."

"It's only Tuesday."

"You know what I mean."

I did. Garrett was a crisis manager. Friday through Sunday were some of his longest days. Monday wasn't

2

much better. By Tuesday, he was able to catch his breath. He usually took Wednesday and Thursday off, which was why our close-knit group of friends met on Tuesday nights for a drink. We were usually busy as hell ourselves the rest of the week anyway.

The others were already waiting for us at the rooftop bar we frequented. It was at the top of the tallest building this side of the city, and you couldn't beat the view. When I first started my career at the age of nineteen, I'd look out at the sprawling city and wonder how the hell I was ever going to get my hands around her throat. I knew I would—I had to—but I didn't know how, or what it would cost me. I just knew that LA didn't have much middle ground, and I wasn't going to sink to the bottom.

Because it wouldn't be just me down there—I'd drag my daughter down with me.

Halley was born when I was nineteen and her mother was seventeen. I hadn't wanted her until they placed her in my arms, and then I'd realized I'd do anything for her. Even take my place in the family business. My dad had started The Walker Agency before I was born. Spent more time tending to it than he did his own family, but the results weren't much better. Just like his family, the company strug- gled. A few boom years followed by long stretches of nothing coming in. Clients leaving him for bigger agencies. A couple of lawsuits. When I was young, it looked to me like he spent most of his time babysitting men who had strong jawlines and no talent, women who had beautiful faces and the magnetism of chalk.

Aside from my mom, my dad had never learned how to pick them.

I quickly learned that I had the opposite problem. Halley's mom was a thorn in my side I'd never fully be able to extract, but I could sense star power from a mile away. It was like a tingling underneath my collar. A tightening in my groin. Lust, but not for the star—for the money he or she would bring me. And Halley.

I'd taken my place in the agency because, let's face it, no one else was offering a nineteen-year-old kid with a high school degree and a newborn a job. But I'd taken to it so well that by the time I was twenty-five and Halley was starting kindergarten, I bought my dad out. By the time I was thirty-one and Halley was going into middle school, I had an A-list agency. When she was in high school, I started taking her to the Oscars with me, which didn't go over well with whatever starlet I was dating. After she went to college, I tried to get her to fly back for awards season, but she was always too busy.

It was wild. My friends hadn't even started their families yet, and here I was with an empty nest. I'd accomplished everything I'd set out to do twenty-one years ago. My daughter was a healthy, happy, thriving adult. I was one of the top five agents in the business. The city was mine.

I toasted it now, something that made my friends laugh. I knew they understood though. She was the white whale we'd all pursued, practically to the point of madness. We'd all sunk our spears deep into her side—almost deep enough to convince ourselves we'd mastered her. Aware she could still thrash the shit out of us if she so chose.

"Here's to money," Garrett said, joining me in the toast.

"And backend compensation," added our friend Dominic, a business manager to the stars. I noticed a Richard Mille Flyback wrapped around his wrist and shook my head. It didn't matter how rich I got, I'd never pay half a mill to know the time.

"And death threats," said Landon, the CEO of the most elite private security firm in LA.

The women at the table behind us turned to stare at him. Smirking, he raised his drink to them.

"And to finding the right actress to play Stasia," Julian said, but he was looking at me rather than the view.

"Shut up," Garrett warned. "I had to drag him out of his office. He was going to look at headshots all night."

"I'll find her," I said to Julian, ignoring Garrett. "I just need some more time."

Julian checked out my face, and then nodded, his mouth tightening as he no doubt reviewed the production schedule in his head. His company had bought the movie rights to a book that the publishing industry referred to as a genre buster. It outsold every other book in its genre a thousand times over. The fan base was massive and rabid. In some ways, that was every producer's dream. A built-in audience. It could be a nightmare too, though. Every single one of those rabid fans had an idea of who they wanted to play Stasia, and the wrong actress could sink the ship.

I'd end up going back to the office tonight. I was close to finding her. I could feel it with the sixth sense I'd discovered when I joined this business. I started to text Maureen that I'd need more headshots on my desk, but then I saw the time was 7:30. She'd gone home for the night. Even though she was seven months pregnant, she'd come back and make sure it got done, but it was a dick move. I didn't mind being a dick in contract negotiations or when it came to telling a client the hard truth, but I made sure I treated my employees well.

Before I could put my phone away, it lit up in my hand. Halley's smiling face appeared. An old picture, from the first time I took her to Disney World when she was seven. The first time since she was born that I felt like I could take a few days off. She was wearing princess mouse ears with her name scrawled across the black dome in hot pink, grinning her old, gap-toothed smile. I smiled back at her for a second before walking a few paces down the balcony and answering it.

"Hey Hals, what's going on?"

"Hi Halley," Garrett yelled from our table.

"Hi, hi," Halley said, her voice bubbly and rushed. "Are you with the Uncles?"

"It's Tuesday night," I said by way of answer.

"Wednesday morning here," she said. She was at our house in Europe with some of her sorority sisters. Croatia, to be exact. I'd looked for a place in Italy, but everywhere I thought I wanted was considered a "hot spot." I wanted to have a place in Europe to *escape* the heat. Then Landon had convinced me to check out Croatia. His family was from there; his grandparents still lived in Zadar. I'd fallen in love with it. Same beautiful blue water, about half the people.

"You have everything you need? The house manager should have stocked the place up before you got there."

"Oh yeah, of course. It's perfect. We love it." Halley sounded distracted though.

"What's up, Hals? You need something?"

I drummed my fingers on the railing. Even though she was twenty-one and well-traveled, I still hated having her so far away. When she went to college on the East Coast, I'd bought her a condo in LA, trying to tempt her back. It hadn't worked. My daughter was independent and fearless. I guess that meant I did something right.

"I sort of do need a favor," she said. "But it's not actually for me."

My eyebrows shot up. Halley hardly ever asked me for favors, and never for other people. She'd learned the hard way about girls who tried to use her to get to me. Had one slipped past her guard? "Oh yeah?"

"It's for Lily. You know? My big sister?"

It took me a second, but I remembered she was referring to the bizarre lingo her sorority used and not to some previously undisclosed half-sister Kim hadn't bothered to tell me about. "Right, I remember her," I said. And I did, vaguely. I had an impression of bright blonde hair and sandy skin. A classic California girl who somehow came from a small town in Ohio. Her mom had been the only person helping her move into the sorority house, and I'd helped her carry in a purple quilted headboard with daisy buttons pinning down the batting. Lily and Halley had gone to Paris together. She was a mainstay in my daughter's updates about her life. I relaxed a little.

"The blonde," Halley added.

"I know it's the blonde," I said. "With the single mom, right?"

"Right. You could still make us sisters, you know."

"That had better not be the favor, Hals." I was glad to hear her joking though. Sometimes Halley didn't think it was funny at all that I couldn't always remember people she'd mentioned or courses she was taking. I didn't think it was that funny either, come to think about it. Just one of the costs I'd wondered about when I set out to conquer this industry. I'd given my daughter the life she deserved and shortchanged her on the family she deserved.

"Oh no, it's much easier than an arranged marriage," Halley assured me. "I was just wondering—do you have any entry level positions at the agency that you think a bright, gorgeous, go-getter like Lily would be right for?" Her voice went up at the end hopefully.

"An entry level position," I repeated, running a hand over the top of my head. Inside it, my thoughts were churning. Had Lily been playing the long game with Halley after all? "What kind of position is she going for exactly? Has she looked at the website?"

"She hasn't yet," Halley's voice trailed off. I knew my daughter well enough to know she had her eyes rolled to the ceiling, one hand tugging at the ends of her dark hair, trying to find the next words to say written in the rafters. "Because she has no idea I'm calling you."

"Hals," I said wearily, but I was relieved that Lily hadn't put Halley up to this. Nothing pissed me off more than people who used my daughter to get to me. It was a cost I hadn't even considered when I set out to become a top agent in the most coveted industry in the country.

"She really needs it, Dad."

I believed Halley because, for one thing, she hardly ever lied to me. And for another, when she was trying to play me, her voice always became wheedling. Now it was quietly matter-of-fact. I stayed quiet while she walked me through how Lily had deferred law school for a year—something she'd apparently already told me, but she didn't get prickly when I didn't remember.

"So she'd need a job and your condo," I surmised when she was done. "Otherwise, every cent I pay her is going to go to rent."

"Yes, which is great since no one is using it anyway."

I had reached the end of the balcony and now I turned back toward my friends. Garrett was staring after me, his hands up in the air. I held up my finger in a *give me a second* gesture and turned back to stare out over the city. I still wasn't completely convinced. If Lily was as smart as Halley said, she knew what a good sob story would impel my soft-hearted daughter to do.

"Please, Dad."

The hope in Halley's voice was clear. Whether Lily was a master manipulator or not, my daughter loved her and wanted this for her. And the only way to find out what Lily really wanted with my daughter was to say yes and watch her closely.

And then drive her back to Ohio at the first sign of trouble.

2

LILY

I stepped out of the Mediterranean stone house onto the back terrace and had to squint against the bright light of the morning sun slanting sideways from the billowing white clouds. This early, the sky wasn't blue yet, but I knew the pale, hazy gold would deepen to cerulean in the next hour. I considered watching the transition from the hammock strung up on the far end of the terrace, but instead I circled the freshwater pool with its light mist of steam rising from the heated water and picked my way down the stone steps to the beach.

"It's not a great beach," my best friend Halley had warned me. "I mean, it's not like Zlatni Rat or Nugal or Sunj. There are no waterfalls, hardly any sand. The water is great, but just, you know, adjust your expectations."

I'd shaken my head in disbelief then, and I did so again now. I couldn't imagine owning this slice of Croatian paradise with its golden pebbled beach and a panoramic view of the Adriatic Sea and feeling the need to *apologize* for it. But Halley had truly been concerned that their group would be disappointed. I couldn't speak for our other three friends, but I was the furthest thing from disappointed. I didn't need to take a day trip to the nudist beach or cliff diving at Punta Verudela—I'd happily spend the entirety of our two-week vacation right here.

Two weeks.

Before the trip, the length had stretched out like a winding golden road that I couldn't see the end of. *Two weeks* to relax and swim and laugh with my friends before I had to deal with the real world. Now that I was a few days in though, suddenly I could see the end too clearly. As always, my mind leapt ahead, gobbling up the time in manageable increments the way it had always done. In the past, my mind had been gobbling up semesters' worth of work, endless shifts at the diner. It had *helped* to break the time down. But now I wanted to stretch the time out.

The knot in my stomach that had loosened the day I turned in her last final and thought *by this time tomorrow, I'll be on a plane to Croatia!* began to tighten again. It never entirely unraveled, not as long as I could remember. I took a deep breath of warm sea-salted air and pressed a hand to my stomach. It would be fine. Everything would be fine. Just because I hadn't gotten the financial aid I'd hoped for and had to defer law school for a year didn't mean anything. It was only a year, after all. My mind went to work on it, breaking it down, reducing it to a series of seasons that would blur by as quickly as senior year had.

But it wouldn't be like senior year at all. I wouldn't have the grants and scholarships that had propelled me through my undergraduate degree. I needed to get a real job and make enough money that I could survive and stockpile for law school. That was going to be hard, and I still had no real idea how to do it. Logically, I should move back in with my mom, but Yellow Springs, Ohio, wasn't exactly rife with economic opportunity. I'd already reached out to law firms in Xenia, Springfield, and Fairborn, but they either weren't looking to hire, or they only had unpaid internships to offer.

The knot tightened further.

I made an abrupt left and walked into the water up to my knees, not even mindful of where I was placing my bare feet. Halley had warned us all about sea urchins, half apologetic again. "Bring water shoes. They're not poisonous, but they'll hurt like a bitch if you step on one."

My racing mind slowed, pleased by the warm water lapping around my ankles and calves, gently nudging at the edge of the sleeveless cotton dress I'd thrown on when I woke up. I smiled down at the shimmering cyan. I could see my outline glittering in the surface. I bent over further so that the ends of my golden hair could trail in the water and took another deep, calming breath. Everything would be fine.

"Are you praying to the sun or something?"

The voice surprised me straight. The wet ends of my hair slapped back against my chest, dampening the cotton dress and chilling my skin beneath. I turned to see Halley standing on the beach—wearing water shoes of course—hands on her hips and a big smile on her face.

"Maybe," I joked, wading back toward the shore. I almost said something like *I can use all the help I can get,* but I bit her tongue just in time. It was no secret that I relied on grants and federal aid to supplement my scholarships, or that I'd deferred law school for financial reasons, but I didn't like to bring it up more than necessary. Especially not to Halley who hadn't even known what a FAFSA was until I explained it to her.

"Should I fill one out too?" Halley had asked, and I had laughed out loud.

"No, your dad owns like half of Hollywood. You won't qualify."

Half of Hollywood, an apartment in Paris that Halley and I had stayed in last summer, a ski chalet that they called a cabin in Aspen, and this beautiful place.

Halley was still grinning when I reached her, a glint of mischief in her dark eyes. I couldn't help smiling back, even though I didn't trust that look. It had gotten us into more trouble than I wanted to remember right now.

"What's up?" I asked, my mind already racing ahead to guess what it might be. She was going to try to talk me into swimming with sharks or cliff diving, or she'd gotten it in her head that we should go to that nudist beach after all.

"Oh nothing," she said in a way that assured me it was definitely something.

I raised my eyebrows at her and waited, a half-smile on my lips even as I began constructing my arguments.

I don't like heights or swimming with creatures that can eat me. I'll take the pictures.

I'll go to the nudist beach, but I'm not going fully nude. No, not even if you buy me unlimited tequila shots.

"Okay, it is something," she said, glee squeezing around her attempt to sound nonchalant. She bounced up on her toes as we began walking back toward the house.

"Something you're going to tell me?" I prodded. Halley didn't usually draw out the suspense like this. She preferred the kamikaze-style attack where she threw everything she had at you so fast your head began spinning and you forgot that *no* was an option. I braced myself for the onslaught of reasons why I *had* to go base jumping or whitewater rafting or whatever dangerous activity she'd set her heart on.

To my surprise, Halley drew in a deep breath and darted me a quick, sideways glance. The glint had dimmed, replaced by a flicker of wariness. She rolled her lower lip beneath her teeth, the way she only did when she was nervous.

I slowed, genuine concern flaring up. I was used to that expression during finals–Halley was a last-minute studier–but never on vacation. "What is it?"

Halley kept walking another few paces, the bounce going out of her step. She knotted her hands in the hem of her gauzy dress, pulling it against her thigh. My concern was edging into worry, but when she turned around, she had a bright smile pasted across her face.

"I've just solved all your problems."

Her voice was bright, but her words landed like darts on the thin skin of my pride. I tried not to flinch. "What problems?" I asked lightly.

She tilted her head in an exasperated, *oh come on* way.

I crossed my arms, hating the sympathy she was trying to conceal.

Halley blew out her breath again. "Lils, I *know* how stressed out you are about having to defer for a year. I know you're still trying to figure out what you're going to do. I know you almost bailed on this trip because you didn't know if you could afford the airfare. And *you* know I'd do anything for you, right?"

"Right," I said stiffly. "But you know I'd never ask you, so I'm not sure–"

"And you *should* know you don't even have to ask me," Halley said, a smile sneaking back across her face. She rocked from her heels to her toes and let go of the hem of her dress, brushing out the wrinkles.

My trepidation built. What had she done? "Halley–" I started.

"It's perfect." Her words rushed over mine. "I can't believe I didn't think of it before."

"*What's* perfect?"

"You need to make money for law school, right? And you're interested in entertainment law, *right?*"

Her voice had hardened with determination, and she was firing the questions like I was on the stand, and she was cross examining the witness.

"I mean I've never said anything about entertainment law, but I'm not opposed to it," I agreed. "But I don't see how that..."

"And you need somewhere to live that isn't going to eat up all the money you're making, *right?*"

Part of me wanted to laugh, but I was too worried about where this line of questioning was leading. I didn't bother answering, just tilted my head and waited for her to get to the point.

"So, what if I told you I knew exactly where you could get a decent paying job for as long as you need it *and* live for free?"

I opened my mouth to answer, but she did it for me.

"You'd say, '*no, Halley. I couldn't possibly.*'" She lowered her voice gravely. "And I'd say, oh come on, Lily, what's the big deal?" She went back into her imitation of my voice again. "And you'd say—"

"Halley!" I cried in exasperation, finally running out of patience. "Get to the point! *What* can't you believe you didn't think of before?"

She blew out her breath. "I called my dad."

In my stomach, the threads of tension turned themselves into a double knot. I groaned out loud; embarrassment and disbelief made my heart palpitate harder in my chest. She'd called her *dad*. "You didn't," I said weakly. "Halley, come on."

"I did," she said, lifting her chin. "And I know you're *so* pissed right now, but I'm not sorry because I was right—he can fix it."

Behind her, the sky was more blue than gold. The beautiful stone house rose up against it, a symbol of everything that Halley had that I never would. I shouldn't be surprised she was trying to force her dad's help on me. All throughout our friendship, she'd wanted to share everything she had with me. We were the sisters the other had never had. Still, there were limits to what I could accept, and Halley had a hard time accepting *that*.

"Call him back," I said finally. "Tell him I already fixed it myself."

She put her hands on her hips again. "Have you?"

No, of course I hadn't. But the real possibility of poverty was better than letting Conall Walker think of me as his daughter's charity case. Unwillingly, I pictured him. He wasn't like the other dads who dropped their daughter off at college in the fall and picked her up in the spring. There was no frayed baseball cap or soft paunch beneath his t-shirt. His hair didn't thin at the top or gray at the temples. He was only forty. Imposingly tall, almost always in dark suits that had been tailored to fit his wide, sculpted shoulders, lean torso, and long legs. Crisp white shirts, shoes that cost more than my college education. Always in dark, frameless sunglasses that hid his eyes and made his expression impossible to read. He never smiled just to be polite, and the few times we'd met, I'd quailed under his direct gaze. Not that he ever really seemed to see me. He only had eyes for his daughter, always making sure she had everything and the best of it at that.

"Don't you want to at least know what I thought of?" Halley wheedled after my prolonged silence confirmed what she already knew. She didn't wait for my answer but plunged ahead. "You're going to have a paid internship with his agency. It's a salaried position, which kind of sucks because you won't get overtime, and believe me you'll work overtime, but you'll have benefits."

A salaried position at Walker Entertainment Agency.

Against my will, my heart beat faster at the possibility. It wasn't a direct line to entertainment law, but I would make good connections. I flattened my lips, trying not to show Halley how interested I was. She grinned triumphantly, knowing me too well to be fooled.

"And," she said with the flair of someone putting a cherry on top of a dessert, "you can stay in my condo for free. It'll just be sitting there after I go back to school in August."

"I have to pay rent," I said automatically.

"There is no rent—it's paid off."

"Then I have to pay the association fee, or whatever," I insisted. "Seriously, Halley. I can't stay there for *free.*"

"Okay fine, you can pay the association fee." She stuck out her hand. "Deal?"

I opened my mouth, then closed it, feeling like I'd been neatly boxed in.

3

CON

I couldn't give Halley's friend an entry level job, big sister or not. We got almost as many applicants for those as we got headshots. Hundreds of people fighting for the opportunity to grasp the bottom rung of the tallest, shiniest ladder. I wasn't above a little nepotism, but since Lily was going to law school in a year, it didn't make sense to give her a job in the mailroom. Instead, I had HR set up an internship that paid just as much as an entry level position, but it had a hard end date. Then I had my house manager prep her condo and asked Maureen to pick the girl up at the airport.

And then I forgot about it.

I had a lot on my plate. The industry was coming back to life after a lean couple of years that had seen productions delayed and projects stopped altogether. I'd finally found Julian's actress for Stasia, but that didn't make a dent in my to do list. Some guys at the top of an agency figured they'd earned the right to coast. They let other people do the pitching and following up and negotiating. I couldn't do it though. Maybe it was because I was younger than some of the other industry vets, but I still wanted to get my teeth in. Leave my mark. Earn my millions. Right now, I was fighting to get one of my actors top billing in a movie he was clearly the star of, but he was playing opposite an established star who felt entitled to it.

There was nothing I hated more than entitlement. I was going to tear into his box office returns and spotlight his latest bad behavior, and if that didn't work, I'd really get my hands dirty. But first, I had to deal with Halley's mother.

Leaving a mountain of work piling up on my desk, I headed across town to Landon's office. He worked strange hours, but I'd made sure he knew I was coming. Everything about his downtown building was designed to create a feeling of discrete security. Heavy, elegant doors that locked automatically behind you. Wide hallways that didn't have any shadowy recesses a stalker could hide in. Soundproof offices so your secrets couldn't escape.

His EA waved me in. "He's been waiting for you."

I nodded tersely and saw her eyebrows elevate slightly as I walked past without a word. Normally I'd stop for pleasantries, but I was on edge today. I didn't like dealing with Kim when I *wasn't* up to my eyeballs in more important shit to do. I couldn't believe I still had to, considering the only thing we had in common besides a distant past was an adult daughter.

"Kim's stirring shit up again," I announced when the heavy door closed behind me with a heavy sigh.

Landon's face stayed neutral. "What does she want?"

"More money."

Only someone who knew Landon as well as I did would have seen the flicker of derision on his face. "Of course she does. She knows the piggy bank is running out of quarters, so she's shaking it one last time."

I nodded, wishing for the hundredth time that I'd insisted on a lump sum payout when my lawyer was negotiating with hers for full custody of Halley. Instead, I'd gotten hooked into paying child support to a woman who hadn't supported our child a day in her life. And worse, I was paying it until Halley graduated from college, so Kim still had another year to shake me down.

"What do you need from me?" Landon asked, steepling his fingers.

"Dirt." I dug my thumb and forefinger into the crevices around the bridge of my nose. "Anything I can use to fend her off. I want proof she's using again. Proof she's charging for blowjobs."

When I looked back at Landon, he was nodding, his face blank.

"I'd just give her a final payment if I thought that would end it," I said.

"I know."

I knew Landon of all people wasn't judging me, but it was a shitty situation overall. Kim had been a pain in my ass for the last two decades, but I still didn't relish what I was asking Landon to do. Not because I had ever really cared about her, but because I loved Halley more than anything.

"I'll see what I can do," Landon said after a minute. His light green eyes squinted at me over his hawk-like nose. His eyebrows came down like storm clouds. "If I can't find anything, what do you want me to do?"

I understood what he was asking immediately. If he didn't find anything, did I want him to plant something? It wasn't in Landon's standard repertoire, but he'd arrange it for me. I considered it for half a second. "No need," I said finally. "If I know Kim, there's something to be found."

Landon nodded, expressionless. My friends knew Kim well. We'd tried to make it work a couple of times when Halley was young. They never liked her, but they didn't say so until we split up for the fourth and final time, right before Halley's fifth birthday. For the past sixteen years, they'd had a front row seat to her bullshit. We all did our best to keep Halley in the dark. She and Kim weren't that close, but they did an annual mother-daughter trip for Halley's birthday every year. I never told her how Kim started pushing for more and more extravagant trips while barely remembering how old Halley was turning.

"She'll be doing this to you too," Landon said as he walked me out. "Keep your nose clean and your ass covered for the next year."

I snorted. Thanks to the twin demands of my career and being a single father, I hadn't had much time to leave a sordid trail for Kim to dig up. "Sure, I'll drop out of the erotic asphyxiation members-only club."

"It's only for a year, pal." Landon clapped me on the back, and we laughed. For a minute, the tension eased in my temples. If I had to have a batshit crazy ex, at least I had a group of friends that had my back no matter what.

After I left his office, I headed uptown for a late lunch with a client. I wasn't looking forward to it. Preston White wanted me to convince Julian to cast him in an upcoming World War 2 epic. I'd told him half a dozen times that Julian wasn't going to take that decision out of the director's hands. Still, I was going to tell him again—this time over a thirty-dollar martini, and I was going to make sure he fucking heard me this time.

"I just think this is *my* role," Preston said for what must have been the thousandth time.

I tipped my own martini back impatiently. I wasn't normally a day drinker, but I needed to take the edge off before I punched Preston in the face or told him what the director really thought of him. The list of adjectives that came back when I put his name forward had been long and unflattering. Pompous, obnoxious, overblown, arrogant. And worst of all, untalented.

"I'm telling you, it's not," I said, putting a note of finality in my voice. "Baz wants an unknown. I can't change his mind. Julian can't change his mind. And you sure as fuck can't change his mind. And if you keep making an ass of yourself, you're going to miss out on the next great role that really is yours."

It had occurred to me more than once during this late lunch that I should just drop Preston and save myself some trouble. It was hard to drop someone whose ask was twenty million and rising though.

While Preston circled back to why he was actually the right person for the role for the hundredth time, I pushed my empty martini glass across the bar and checked my phone. To my surprise, I'd missed three calls in a row from Halley.

"Hold on a second," I said, cutting Preston off midstream. I got off the barstool and walked to an empty corner of the bar to call her back. I was relieved when she answered immediately, sounding fine.

"Hey, is something wrong?" I asked anyway. It wasn't like her to call multiple times.

"Oh, yeah, of course," she said like she couldn't fathom why I'd worry. She didn't understand it was a habit I'd developed when I was younger than she was now, trying to raise a two-year-old on my own. "I was just calling because no one picked up Lily at the airport."

I frowned and checked my messages. I'd missed a call from Maureen, too, and a text that told me she'd had to go to the hospital. Contractions. Another text telling me not to worry, false alarm. Fucking Preston, distracting me. "Tell her to take a cab," I said to Halley. "The company will reimburse her."

Across the bar, Preston was ordering another martini. The fucker. I wasn't going to watch him marinate in gin all afternoon. I made a throat slashing motion to the bartender when his back was turned and missed what Halley was saying. Something about making Lily feel welcome.

"I'm making her feel welcome," I countered. "With a job most new college graduates would kill for and a free place to live in one of the most expensive cities in the world."

"*Dad*," Halley huffed. "Don't throw our privilege in her face. I told her you were glad she was coming. Making her take a cab doesn't exactly say *welcome to LA.*

"Well the job and condo don't exactly say *get the fuck out*," I replied, ignoring the bit about privilege. But I already knew it was a lost cause. My daughter could harangue me like no pompous, obnoxious, arrogant, over-blown actor ever could. Besides, it was a reason to get out of this interminable lunch. I spoke over whatever indignant diatribe Halley was delivering. "I'm on my way."

Luckily my office was only a few blocks from lunch. I went straight to the valet stand and was on the road within minutes. Not that it mattered. Rush hour traffic in LA was practically an all-day affair. It took me a while to get to the Westchester area. I used the time to make a few follow up calls. Somehow, soothing neurotic actors and telling them I was sure their audition had blown the fucking socks off whoever they were auditioning for made the drive go by relatively quickly. Before I knew it, I was standing in the terminal.

I glanced around impatiently for someone standing alone. All I saw were a few families, a student group, some couples, and what had to have been a model or an aspiring actress. A tall, sunny, gorgeous blonde in tight jeans and a short, loose shirt that didn't hide the generous curves of her breasts. There were so many skinny, flat-chested models in LA that a woman with curves was a refreshing sight. I eyed her speculatively as I called Halley. When she picked up, I asked, "Where the hell is Lily? If she took a cab after all…"

"She said she'd be by the coffee shop."

"Well she isn't."

The model/actress pushed back long, wheat-colored hair. Her short-sleeved shirt rose up, revealing a slice of flat, tan stomach. An actress, I decided. She had too much shape to be a model. An hour-glass figure, like one of the fifties starlets. Landon had told me to keep my nose clean, but that didn't mean I couldn't talk to a woman, did it?

Exasperated, Halley said, "Yes, she is. I just texted her. She's wearing a gray shirt and dark jeans, she has a red suit-case, and she's standing right underneath the sign. You can't miss her."

Just then, the blonde lifted her eyes from her phone to mine.

A punch of lust followed by a nasty shock went through me.

The beautiful woman was Lily.

4

———

LILY

Halley's dad looked mad.

I had the impression of a cat that had been dunked in water and come up spitting. Confusion, surprise, and then anger had crossed his face in a matter of seconds. Now it was smoothing out, becoming the blandly charming expression I remembered from our college move-in days. He strode toward me, sliding his phone back into his coat pocket.

"Apologies, Lily. I didn't see you there."

He had, though. I'd felt him notice me. I hadn't realized it was him, but I'd felt eyes sweeping over me with that sixth sense every girl had. "No, I'm the one who should apologize," I said, trying to regain a sense of equilibrium. "I should have just taken a cab." I was too embarrassed to admit that I'd been intimidated by the idea. Overwhelmed. That I almost would have rather booked a flight back to Ohio and spent the summer

"No, you shouldn't have," Halley's dad said smoothly, picking up my suitcase as though it held air instead of everything I owned. "I'd never have heard the end of it from my daughter."

I laughed nervously and fell into step beside him. "I can
—" I gestured toward the suitcase.

He snorted and didn't bother responding. I felt unbe-
lievably tongue tied as we walked in silence to his sleek
black Mercedes that probably cost twice what my law
degree would. God, I wished Halley was there. I took a
deep breath and thought about my bubbly friend who
seemed to have never met a stranger. What would she do in
this situation?

She'd talk. Breathless sentences, stories that required
hardly any audience participation. She'd laugh at herself
and make whoever else was there laugh too. I rallied every
bit of my nerve and started talking.

It worked, sort of. The terrible silence was broken at
least as I told him all about my flight and how excited I was
to be in LA and how I was *so* grateful but also embarrassed
because Halley never should have called him, but God he
was saving my life.

Halley's dad nodded, grunted, and smiled in the right
places, but I could tell he was only half listening. I had a
feeling he was used to slipping into autopilot like this. That
was fine with me. I kept one eye on the GPS, watching the
time elapse and the distance shrink. I burbled so much that
I was thirsty by the time we slipped beneath the city into a
parking garage. I hadn't even noticed the building above it,
I'd been so busy talking, but Halley had shown me pictures.
I knew a sleek glass building grew tall against the skyline
and that from her long, narrow balcony, I'd be able to see
the long blue rectangle of the pool surrounded by lounge
chairs and planted palm trees.

Despite myself, I started to feel excitement flicker
through the nerves I'd felt ever since I boarded the plane. I
looked over at Halley's dad and smiled. He was already

getting out of the car, though. The trunk rose behind us, and I saw his large shoulders flex with the effort. So it wasn't weightless to him after all. I slid out of the car and shouldered my large purse, extending my free hand again.

"Thank you so much—"

"I'll walk you in," he said. He'd taken off his sunglasses when we entered the parking garage, and now I could see his eyes—so dark I couldn't see where the pupils became the iris. God, he was handsome. And there was something devilish in the severity of his pale skin against his black hair and eyes. Halley never tanned either.

Halley.

The reminder of my best friend was like icy water splashing in my face. I couldn't be checking out her dad. She had nothing but derision for the few women he'd dated while he was raising her. I'd always had a feeling that had more to do with not wanting to share her dad's attention than anything wrong with the women.

"You don't have to walk me in," I tried to insist, but I don't even know if he heard me. He had turned away and started walking toward the elevator. I had to walk quickly to catch up. The ride to the 30th floor was excruciatingly long. Did he really have to have bought Halley a condo on the top floor? Finally, the elevator doors slid open, revealing a hallway that seemed like it belonged in a five-star hotel. Natural light flooded in from floor-to-ceiling windows on either end of the hallway. It made the wide gray planks of the floor gleam like a dark river running between the cream-colored walls. I followed Halley's dad as he turned left and walked to the far end. He shifted my suitcase into his left hand and pulled a key fob out of his pocket. I saw the pad flicker from red to green, and then he was pushing open the door.

I think I literally gasped when I followed him in and saw the view, but again he acted as though he hadn't heard me. He moved quickly, efficiently, setting my suitcase on the inside of the door to the main bedroom and then giving me a quick tour.

"Kitchen, living room, office," he checked them off in clipped tones, hardly looking at them himself. I couldn't stop looking. With the exception of maybe his apartment in Paris, I'd literally never been in a place this nice. The neutral gray flooring continued from the outer hallway throughout the floorplan. The kitchen was small, but even I recognized that the appliances were top of the line and the counter was white granite with silver and gold veins shot through. Barstools with thick gold legs and white cushions sat at the bar in lieu of a table. There was an overstuffed pink couch—the biggest spot of color—in the living room, facing the wall that had a flatscreen TV mounted above a long electric fireplace.

I peeked in at the office, which had a full-sized bed against the window and a desk against the wall. When I looked back, Halley's dad was standing in the kitchen, looking impatient. He quickly wiped the expression from his features, but I was sure I saw it. My nerves flared up again, and I went into bubbly overdrive.

"Thank you *so* much, again, uh..." I floundered, realizing I had no idea what to call him. In my head, he was always *Halley's dad*. Should I call him Mr. Walker? He was going to be my boss after all. But that sounded strange and stiff, like he was as old and grumpy and not...well, hot.

"Call me Con," he said wryly, like he was reading my thoughts.

My face flushed, hoping he couldn't really. "Great, thank you so much, Con." I moved toward him, my sorority party training taking over. Before I could think better of it, I was moving in for a hug. I saw the flicker of surprise on his face, but it was too late to pull out of it. My arms wrapped around his rock-solid midsection. His arms spread, then he rested his hands gingerly on my arms for about half a second before easing back.

"Let Halley know if you need anything," he said, retreating down the hall. He'd slid his sunglasses back down over his eyes so I couldn't see his expression. I wished I had something to hide behind, too. I was overcome, first with mortification for hugging him, and then with a breathless sensation of my body tingling everywhere it had come into contact with his.

Even after I heard the door close behind him, I stood in the kitchen for a long time, my thoughts a maelstrom of confusion, embarrassment, and lust all combined, making me feel anxious and strangely excited, and then, suddenly exhausted. I walked into the living room and dropped down on the overstuffed pink sofa. It was the only thing in the condo that felt like Halley. That and the chunky knit blanket hanging over the arm. Halley was always cold. I wasn't, but I pulled it over me anyway, the cocoon helping to calm my racing heart.

It was going to be a long year.

* * *

I must have fallen asleep because when my phone began vibrating on the glass coffee table, it jolted me awake. I pushed the blanket back and sat up, reaching for it. I was glad to see Halley's name on FaceTime, the picture of us at spring break in Miami last year grinning back at me.

"Guess where I am?" I said when I picked up.

"In my condo!" she squealed, seeing it behind me. "It's

so cool to have you there. It makes me want to come visit you."

"You mean visit yourself," I said with a laugh.

"No, no. It's *your* condo for the next year," she corrected herself. "I'll stop calling it mine."

"You can call it yours, Halley. It definitely isn't mine." I stood up, taking her with me out onto the balcony. I could see for miles, and it seemed like the pool below was a mile away itself. I'd never been afraid of heights, but I took a step away from the railing anyway. No point in taking chances. "How's senior year going?"

"Good! Everyone says hi." She raised the phone so I could see a gaggle of sisters spread out over the bright green lawn. They waved from their blankets and beach towels. I felt a pain of longing twist in my heart. In the excitement of the move to LA, I hadn't had much time to think about what was happening at school. Move-in day, the welcome back festivities in the square, the beginning-of-the-year parties that were only matched by the end-of-year parties. Halley pulled the phone back in so I could only see her face framed by the brilliant blue sky. "Is my dad taking care of you?"

I pictured her dad's impassive face. Felt his body against mine again. A flush rose to my cheeks. "Yes," I said, and started coughing. My throat had gone dry. I went back inside and filled a glass with water. "Yes," I repeated after I swallowed. "He's great."

"You're lying," Halley laughed. "I know my dad. He probably was on his phone the entire time and threw you out at the curb. Just tell me, Lily. I'll yell at him right now."

"No," I said quickly. "He wasn't on his phone at all. And he carried my suitcase up. Seriously, he's been great."

I wandered into the bedroom and saw my suitcase sitting on the inside of the door where he had left it. He had probably wanted to get on his phone, but I'd kept up an incessant chatter the entire way. I wanted to groan out loud, but then Halley would *really* call him up to find out what he'd done.

"Tell me about school," I ordered Halley. "I miss everything so much."

She heard the sincerity in my voice and pulled a sympathetic face. "It's great, but I wish you were here." Then she launched into a minute-by-minute account of the first week that made me laugh and forget about my embarrassment. By the time we got off the phone, the sky was darkening in the east. I had a feeling that if I was facing west, there would be a spectacular sunset on display. I walked out onto the balcony with a glass of chardonnay I found in the refrigerator and settled into one of the wicker egg chairs. I pulled my feet up into the cushion and inhaled the crisp, nearly acidic scent of the drink. It looked fancy. Probably cost as much as my plane ticket. I made a mental note of the label with the half-hearted hope that I could replace it.

In two days, I would officially start my post-college life. I took a deep sip of the lip-puckeringly dry wine and wished it was one of the cheap white wines we used to buy by the gallon. The evening was beautiful. The condo behind me was luxurious. I was about to start an internship people would kill for. But for some reason, as I thought about the man who had made it all possible, I felt a strange longing. It didn't make any sense to feel that way about him. He was *Halley's dad.* Yes, he was intimidatingly good looking, but he was so far out of reach that it didn't make sense to feel like I had lost out on something. I shouldn't feel my heart beat faster or desire curl in my belly when I pictured the laconic twist of his lips. I shouldn't want to know how his thick, dark hair would feel between my fingers, or remember the way his body felt pressed against mine with anything but embarrassment.

What would Halley think?

But that antidote had lost its potency. It didn't do a thing to lessen the inexplicable longing in my chest for a man I could never have.

For the first time, the thought of my best friend only made me feel lonelier.

5

CON

Naturally, Kim hired a hack to tail me. I spotted the dumb fuck immediately. He was parked just outside the gates of my community, and he didn't even give me a head start before pulling onto the road behind me. I gave him a curt wave in the rearview mirror to let him know I knew what he was doing. He had the nerve to wave back, and I saw a grin creep across his wide face, the corners of his mouth pushing his cheeks up into round scoops.

I shook my head in disgust. Leave it to Kim to hire some cheap ass PI who would tail me on the freeway and ask my clientele for autographs. I had half a mind to call her up and offer her a hundred grand to get someone less obtrusive. The moron tailed me all the way to work, even trying to follow me into the parking garage beneath my building.

"Don't let that guy in," I said briefly to Frank, the garage attendant. "My ex-wife hired him to dig up dirt on me."

Frank nodded, unfazed. He was used to all kinds of strange requests. He'd been working in LA since the 70s.

Instead of taking the elevator straight to the executive floor like I usually did, I stopped in the lobby. The woman behind the desk widened her eyes in surprise when I approached, and I realized that I couldn't remember the last time I'd been down here. Even on my way out, I took the side alley exit the actors used to avoid paparazzi.

"Good morning." I glanced at her badge, but it was turned around. "I wanted to make sure that everything was set up for an intern who is starting today."

She reached for a stack of folders and flipped through them quickly. I knew I was making her nervous and wondered what the hell had happened. When I first bought out my dad and made the company my own, I'd made sure to know everyone. There were company happy hours that included everyone from the mailroom to the top tier management. Now I'd become as disengaged as my dad had been. I made a mental note to fix this later, when Kim was off my back.

"Lily Anderson?" She pulled a blue folder out from the middle of the stack. "One-year internship? Starting in brand consulting?"

"That's the one. Is everything ready for her?"

"Yes, sir. As soon as she gets here, we'll—"

"I'm here!"

The now-familiar bright lilt of Lily's voice sounded behind me. I stiffened, wishing I'd gone straight to my office at all. Unexpectedly, the memory of her body pressing up against mine played in my head again. Her generous curves brushing against my chest, her slender arms slipping around my waist. I could feel her soft hair brushing my throat and chin again, smell the notes of vanilla perfume that clung to her skin.

Unwillingly, I turned around to face her. She was wearing a lavender dress that she'd dressed up with a blazer and heels. She looked professional, except that the sunlight streaming in behind her made her gauzy skirt filmily transparent. I could see the outline of her shapely thighs, the curve of her hips. My mouth went dry when she smiled, so sunnily innocent of what she was doing to me.

Nothing. She was doing *nothing* to me. I tightened my mouth. "Good morning. I was just making sure everything was ready for you. Lily Anderson, this is..."

Shit. I still didn't know.

"Helena Upchurch." The receptionist said immediately when I hesitated. She rose and held out her hand to Lily. "Pleased to meet you. I'll let security know you're here."

"Security?" Lily's eyes widened and sought mine.

"For your badge," I said tightly. Why did she keep looking at me with those wide, appealingly blue eyes like I was saving her from something? I wasn't here to be her knight in shining fucking armor. I rapped my knuckles on the desk, an old habit. I'd worked to break it ever since Griffin told me it was my tell in poker. "Whenever you feel backed into a corner, you start tapping." Then I'd realized I did it in contract negotiations too. And apparently Lily was making me feel backed into a corner now.

"I have to go," I said abruptly. "Helena, you can take it from here, right?"

The dark-haired woman nodded smartly. I nodded goodbye to Lily, who smiled and started to thank me again, but I was already moving away. When the elevator doors closed behind me, I breathed out an irritable sigh of relief. I hadn't felt this itchy around a woman in a long time. Generally, it was straight forward. If she caught my interest, I went after her. When my interest waned, I broke it off. Between the business and my daughter, I didn't have time to waste being the nice guy when my heart wasn't in it. And I could count on one hand how many women kept my interest long enough for me to introduce them to Halley.

Alone in the elevator, I could admit to myself that Lily had caught my attention. I wasn't sure why. Yes, she was beautiful, but I worked in LA. There were beautiful women everywhere I looked. There was an innocence about her, a naivete. The hug, for example. With any other woman, I'd have assumed it was calculated. I'd have laughed and stepped away because the rules of the game would have been clear. But with Lily, I didn't get any sense of artifice. She had hugged me because I'd been helping her, because I was her best friend's dad. Not because she expected the gesture to go straight to my dick.

The problem was, I couldn't follow my usual routine. Lily had caught my attention, but I couldn't do jack shit about it. And I definitely couldn't do what I normally did—sleep with her. It was a surefire way for me to lose interest, but she was practically a kid, only a year older than my daughter. Her *little sister*, in sorority language.

A small tingle of disgust wormed its way up in my throat. It wasn't as good as disinterest, but it was a start. I berated myself the rest of the way to my office, trying to solidify this feeling. Trying to forget the way the sun turned her hair into gold and rendered her dress all but transparent.

For the majority of the morning, I was successful. I was still haggling over top billing for one of my clients, and I was trying to convince a major studio to cast a relative unknown in a big part—never an easy proposition.

"You said yourself she did the best read," I said to the producer, snapping my pen against my desk the way I only did when I was *this* close to biting someone's head off. "I signed her myself. You think I waste my time on anyone who isn't the cream of the crop?"

"She's not pretty," the man on the other end said bluntly. "She can act her ass off, but her face is still..." he paused, looking for a diplomatic way to put it. "Not pretty," he finally repeated.

"Not pretty?" I spat, smacking my pen against the glass desktop so loud that Maureen turned around in her chair to look at me. I held up a hand, letting her know everything was fine, and lowered my voice. "I must have missed something in the script. What do her looks have to do with inspiring a worker's revolution in early twentieth century America?"

"Everything in America has to do with looks," he said drolly, unimpressed by my self-righteous anger. "Especially when it gets put on a billboard in Times Square."

"You're a fucking idiot if you don't cast her, Pierre."

I could practically hear his shrug over the phone. I tightened my grip on my pen. I had to find another angle, or he would cast a Kardashian in the role, and my client would be back to playing second fiddle in another rom com. I'd promised her better. I cleared my throat and relaxed my voice. "Let's do this over lunch. When are you free?"

He sighed. "I don't know. I'll ask my assistant to get in touch with yours and set something up."

"Something this week," I specified. I wouldn't put it past him to schedule something for next month, after the role had already been given to someone else and principal photography began.

"Something this week," he agreed grudgingly. "But I—"

"Great." I hung up the phone before he could attach any conditions, then I called Maureen. She picked up and swiveled around in her chair again to look at me through the glass. She had a hand resting on her very pregnant stomach, reminding me that I needed to get a temp in as soon as possible, especially after the false alarm the other day. "Get in touch with Pierre's assistant today," I ordered. "Get a lunch on the books as soon as you can. He's trying to fuck over Sienna Birch for that factory fire movie."

Maureen shook her head disapprovingly. She was as invested in our clients as I was. "I'm on it."

I leaned back in my chair and stretched my arms over my head, adrenaline pumping through my veins. I could visualize Sienna in that role so clearly that I knew there was no other option. She would elevate an already great script, and the success would elevate her into strong character roles. Pierre wasn't wrong about her looks. She'd never be the traditional leading lady, but she had talent to spare.

When my phone rang and I saw it was Maureen, I picked up eagerly. I expected her to tell me the lunch was on the books. To my surprise, she said, "Halley is on line one."

I glanced at the clock. 11:15. If I remembered her schedule correctly, Halley should be leaving her morning class. "Hey Hals, what's up?" I asked when Maureen connected us. "Why didn't you call my cell?"

"I wanted to talk to Maureen first."

I raised my eyebrows. "Oh yeah? What about?"

"Your schedule." Halley all but hummed the words, making me instantly suspicious.

"What about my schedule, Hals?"

"I thought it would be nice if you took Lily to lunch if you were free. Which, by the way, you are."

I glared at Maureen's back, even though there was no way she could have known. "Why would I take Lily to lunch?" I asked, trying to keep annoyance out of my voice. The last thing I wanted to do was sit across from the woman I was trying *not* to think about, making bullshit conversation about fuck knows what. It wasn't like we had anything in common other than Halley, and I sure as hell didn't want to think about that.

But Halley was prepared for that question, and she launched into a five-minute diatribe about how Lily was her *best* friend, and she didn't know a soul, and wouldn't I want someone to take her to lunch if she were in Lily's place?

Not someone like me, I thought.

"It's a bad idea, Hals," I said. "She needs to make friends with people here. Going to lunch with the boss looks like special treatment. Besides, she probably already has plans. Brand development is a friendly group."

They were vipers, but it wasn't my problem. Lily was only going to be with them for two months before her internship rotated to media rights.

"She doesn't have plans," Halley said so positively that my suspicion level jumped even higher.

"How do you know?"

"Because I told her that you wanted to take her to lunch!" Halley's voice filled with artificial cheer. "Well, I've got to go. Thanks for making my *best friend* feel welcome, Dad. You're the best. Love you tons. Byeeee!"

She disconnected before I could even draw in breath to start yelling at her. I slammed the receiver down in the base and shoved back from my desk, ready to go find *someone* to direct my pent-up frustration at.

But before I could figure out who, Lily was standing in my doorway.

6

LILY

If I'd thought he looked mad before at the airport, it's only because I hadn't seen him *really* mad. Right now, with his black brows slanted together and his face so tight that the skin stretched over his bones, he looked positively fearsome.

I took a step back, regretting it already. I knew it was a bad idea, but Halley had been so insistent. Her coaxing words came back to haunt me. "Oh, come on, Lily. He really wants to take you to lunch. No, he is not intimidating. He's my dad! That means, as my big sister, he's practically *your* dad."

I'd nearly swallowed my tongue then. "No, he isn't!"

But she'd laughed and coaxed and of course I'd gotten off the phone with her, completely convinced that I'd read Con all wrong and that he really did want to take me to lunch. Now I realized that my first impression had been right. I should have eaten alone at my cubicle after the cliquey, narrow-eyed, whispering crew of Brand Development left for the lunch they planned next to my desk without inviting me.

"I'm sorry," I said instinctively. I wasn't sure what I was

apologizing for, but in my experience, when someone looked at you like that, it was because you'd done something terribly wrong.

Con's eyebrows lowered further. "For what?" he asked, sounding as mad as he looked.

"For..." I gestured uncertainly. "I'm not sure, I guess." I laughed out of pure nervousness. "You just look really angry."

I could tell I'd surprised him because for a minute, he just stared at me. Then his features relaxed, and he even gave me a reluctant half-smile. "I am, but it's not because of you."

"Oh, well, if this is a bad time..." I was already backing up another step. I'd be so happy to eat alone in my cubicle. Thrilled to watch the others file out without me. Anything to avoid spending an hour alone with this intense, darkly handsome man who always seemed on the verge of anger.

"No, it's not." His voice snapped out like a whip, stopping me in my tracks. He glanced at the clock. "I have an hour."

"Great," I said weakly. An hour. How on earth was I going to sit across from him for an hour? Nervousness burbled up in my throat as we walked back to the elevator in silence. This was like the car ride all over again, but worse. He didn't have traffic to distract him, and I didn't have a GPS ticking down the minutes to stare at.

I cursed Halley again when we walked down the block to a restaurant I couldn't afford in a million years. "You're not a vegetarian, are you?" Halley's dad asked, frowning.

I shook my head, half wishing I was. This place looked nicer than the steakhouse my mom had taken me to after my college graduation. Halley had come with us and called it so cute. Now I could see why. Morton's Steakhouse did look like a cute younger sibling, dressing up in its big brother's clothes compared to this place.

The front desk was manned by a maître d' instead of a host, and he knew Con immediately. "Mr. Walker, Maureen just called to let us know you'd be dining with us today. We have your table ready."

The place was airy but intimate. The booth he took us to was tucked into a corner, discreetly hidden from view of the entrance. I slid in and murmured my thanks when he handed me a leather-bound menu. I opened it, hoping there would be an appetizer or side that I could order for my meal without looking conspicuous.

There were two narrow pieces of cream paper secured to the leather folio with gold bands in each corner. One side was entirely dedicated to wine and whiskey, priced by the bottle, and the numbers made my stomach drop even before I even looked at the food. When I did, it was worse than I expected. The least expensive item was the starter Caesar salad for twenty-five dollars. The most expensive was a steak that came in just under a hundred dollars, but that didn't include sides.

Con must have sensed my shock because he said without looking up from his own menu, "This is on the company. We take every new employee out for lunch."

I wasn't sure I believed him, but the knots in my stomach loosened slightly. I ordered the least expensive entrée and water. I didn't hear what Con ordered because I was too busy trying to think of what I could ask him to prevent another awkward silence from falling between us. I'd just decided that I'd ask him how he started his own agency when I realized that the waiter was gone and Con was staring at me.

He'd said something, but I couldn't for the life of me figure out what it was.

"I said, how did you and Halley become friends?" he repeated, a small smirk curling the edge of his mouth in a way that made his face look the opposite of friendly.

"We met at rush week," I said, latching onto the topic happily. Of course we should talk about Halley. It was the only thing we had in common. "She was a freshman fall rush. I became her Big."

"I have to admit, I was surprised when she wanted to join a sorority." Con took a sip of water, his eyes latched onto mine over the rim.

I bristled. I'd heard that tone a dozen times before. A seemingly innocuous comment except that it was underlined with derision. "Why is that?" I asked, keeping my voice bright and upbeat with effort.

He shrugged his broad shoulders negligently. "I just didn't think she was the sorority girl type."

"The sorority girl type?" I repeated, still determined not to let annoyance creep into my voice. I couldn't be annoyed with Con. He was my boss, he was paying for this lunch, and most importantly, he was Halley's dad. "I'm not sure what you mean."

"Vapid," he said bluntly. "More concerned with parties and boys—" here his lip curled down "—than going to class."

I took a sip of my own water, cooling the hot words that wanted to spring to my lips. He watched me carefully, and I had the feeling he was amused. "I think you've gotten the wrong idea about sororities," I finally said with as much saccharine sweetness as I could hold on my tongue without gagging. "Probably because you're in an industry that doesn't really understand the bonds of sisterhood and therefore reduces women to bimbos and sluts."

He raised one eyebrow laconically. "Well please, enlighten me."

This part was easy. I could list a dozen ways that sororities were beneficial. The hard part was keeping the irritation out of my voice when he was so clearly trying not to smirk. "Some sororities might focus on parties and boys, but not all. Ours was about community. We did volunteer work and held fundraisers. It's about learning to be a leader. I was the vice president, so I basically learned how to run a household of forty girls, which taught me about budgeting and conflict resolution..."

I kept going until the waiter came by with our meals. He slid them in front of us and stood back politely, waiting for a break in my diatribe.

"And of course, the networking," I finished up. "If not for the sorority, I might not have met Halley, and I wouldn't be sitting here right now."

I sat back, my heart beating fast. I wasn't mad exactly, just passionate. My cheeks felt flushed, and my mind was already jumping ahead, anticipating his possible responses even as I murmured to the waiter that I didn't need anything else.

Con inclined his head, and the man walked away. Another silence fell, but this one didn't feel as awkward. He was watching me with something like speculative interest, like I'd surprised him. And instead of saying anything snarky, he said, "Okay, you've convinced me."

My mouth dropped open. "Just like that?"

He raised his wrist and looked at his watch ironically.

The flush worked its way to my cheeks. "I have a lot to say about the topic," I said defensively. "You wouldn't believe what people will say to your face when they find out you're in a sorority."

"I can only imagine." Con's lips twisted wryly. "It's good preparation for what people are willing to say to your face in this town."

There was an exasperated note in his voice that told me

he wasn't just speaking off the cuff. I tilted my head, waiting for the story.

He shook his head. "It's about an actress I'm trying to get in a movie, but it's not something I can talk about really. Not yet. I can't risk it leaking."

I looked around as ostentatiously as he'd looked at his watch. "I don't see anyone hiding in the potted plants," I said.

He smiled again, and this time it was the closest thing to a real smile I'd seen yet. "Another time, maybe. But suffice to say, I'm glad that Halley never wanted to go into this industry."

I looked up at him in surprise, wondering if he was joking. Halley absolutely wanted to go into this business.

His gaze sharpened. "What?"

He wasn't joking. I bit the inside of my lip, wondering how to pull my shoe out of what I'd just stepped in. "It's just," I fumbled, "I'm surprised because isn't this a family business? I thought maybe you'd want Halley to take over the agency eventually."

It was a good recovery, if not also wildly untrue. I'd never once heard Halley talk about joining the agency. She didn't want to negotiate contracts; she wanted to be in front of the camera. I couldn't believe he didn't know.

"A family business," he repeated, dark eyes narrowed on mine like he knew there was something I wasn't telling him. A long, pregnant pause followed. Nervous words bubbled to the back of my tongue, but I swallowed them back. I didn't trust myself not to spill everything if I let the bubbly autopilot take over. I swallowed nervously and tried to smile. His expression didn't crack. I had the feeling I was on the losing end of one of his hardball negotiations, but I *couldn't* lose. I didn't know what Halley's reasons were for keeping her ambition a secret from the parent she was so close to, but she must have a good one.

"Yes," I said finally through my smile. "Your dad started it, right?"

I'd met Halley's grandfather more times than I'd met Con when we were undergraduates. I guess because he was retired and had plenty of free time, whereas Con always seemed to be pulling himself away from work with great difficulty. He liked to take us out to dinner and tell us all about the agency's latest successes. For the first year I knew her, I thought that *he* was still the owner.

I got the feeling I'd said something else wrong though, from the way Con's brows lowered. "The company I joined was very different from what it is today. My father's company had six employees total and barely covered their overhead. Today, the Walker Agency is in every top five list in this industry."

I could tell I had struck a nerve, but for once, I didn't care. Anything to take his focus off Halley.

"Of course," I said. "But your dad still started it, right? I mean he's the original Walker."

"Technically," he said grudgingly.

A silence followed. I finished my steak salad and shook my head when the waiter came by with the water pitcher.

"Just the check," Con said. His words were clipped, but his face had relaxed.

I looked away when he signed it, not wanting to see the total. Then I followed him back out onto the busy avenue. The sun was blazing brightly above, but a soft wind blew the burn out of the heat. There were more people out now, and I had to walk closer to him to keep from running into oncoming pedestrians. The crowd seemed to part around him even as eyes slid to the edges of their sockets to watch him go. It wasn't just the women; men were compelled by him too. He radiated some mysterious X factor that went beyond his looks and understated wealth. It was a gravity, a power, like he was the center of something and those in his orbit were helpless to do anything but revolve around him.

Halley had charisma, but this was something different.

I shivered, despite the warmth of the day, but when we reached The Walker Agency, I was surprised to find I was disappointed. The moment I'd been anticipating since I found myself in this predicament was here. All I had to do now was say *thanks so much for lunch* and we'd go our separate ways. If Halley was done twisting his arm, I might not spend another minute alone with him for the rest of the year. He was a busy man, after all.

His expression was lighter as though he were having the same thought. "I'm going to drop you off here," he said, slowing to a stop in front of the building. "I have some business on the other side of town."

I heard a note of dark relish in his voice, like he was looking forward to twisting someone's arm until they were forced to see something his way. It was ominous, but a thrill went through me all the same. What was wrong with me? I'd never been attracted to someone like Con before. My friends had loved the dark, brooding guys, but I'd always wanted the bright, sunny ones. The ones who made you laugh instead of squirm, who got along easily with my mom.

But I had to admit, I'd never been attracted to them for long.

I'd certainly never been in love.

I shaded my eyes with my hand and looked up at Con, my heart beating unexpectedly fast. "Thank you for lunch," I said breathlessly.

"Of course," he said automatically, then almost as an afterthought, "I always take new employees out for a welcome-to-the-agency lunch."

There was no way that was true. I was sure of it now. He was far too busy to take out every mail clerk and intern who rotated through. His eyes met mine, and lust speared through me.

Before I could stop myself, I moved toward him.

7

CON

Acting on pure instinct, I held my hand up to ward Lily off. She hesitated, her cornflower blue eyes widening. The sunlight was gilding her again, refracting off the small diamond studs in her earlobes. Her pink lips were curved in a smile, and her cheeks were rosy from the brisk pace I'd set on the walk here. She looked blindingly beautiful, and achingly young. For a second, I wished I hadn't stopped her. I wanted to feel her slim arms slip around me, but not just for a platonic hug. I wanted her to tilt her head back and press the full length of her body against mine, to taste her lips to see if they were as soft as they looked.

It made me irrationally angry, and my voice came out harsher than I intended. "Lily, this isn't a sorority. In the real world, you shake hands with someone to say goodbye instead of rubbing up against them."

Her smile dissolved instantly as her flower petal lips parted in surprise. The roses in her cheeks darkened to crimson and spread across her face. The sparkle in her eyes dimmed.

I tried to soften my voice, but I could still hear the bite

in it. "I'm telling you this for your own good. You don't want to give people the wrong idea in this industry."

"I'm sorry," she said, her voice so tight it was like her vocal chords were strangling the syllables.

"Don't be sorry," I barked, inexplicably annoyed by her apology. "Just be smarter."

I hadn't said it to piss her off, but when her lips clamped together and her eyes narrowed, I realized I'd done just that. Good. I preferred her anger to her hurt. A second ago it felt like I'd just kicked Bambi, but now the light of battle was in her eyes. I'd seen it there when she was defending sorority life, too, and I liked it. It made me want to—

No. I cut my thoughts off at the knees and turned away from her. It was a shitty way to say goodbye, but the more distance I got from her, the better I felt. My head cleared. I could breathe again.

Maybe it had been cruel, but it had been necessary. At least, that's what I told myself.

***Cruel but necessary became the theme of my day. Preston called and tried to pressure me into strongarming Julian into forcing the producer to cast him. I didn't even try to couch my disdain, telling him in no uncertain terms what I'd do if he bothered me one more fucking time about this role that he wasn't fucking good enough for, that he'd never be good enough for. And when he threatened to find a new agent, I laughed.

"Go ahead," I said. "Enjoy being the B-list version of Matthew McConaughey."

Then, fired up from that interaction, I called the agent of the actor who wanted top billing over my guy. I knew some sordid shit about his that wouldn't play well in the media.

"If you leak to the media, you'll sink the entire production," the agent snapped, but I heard the quaver beneath his words.

"So?" I countered. "I'll get my guy the lead in the next Michael Bay movie while yours gets knocked back to playing murder victim number two on CSI."

A furious silence burned up the line, and I knew I'd won.

You'd think I'd have been in a good mood by the time I met up with my friends for happy hour, but for some reason, discontent still seethed in my veins. I tipped back my drink faster than usual and tried to relax while Garrett bitched about the latest predicament one of his most troublesome clients had gotten into. I laughed with the others when he told us how he tried to bribe the LAPD and nearly gotten arrested himself, but it felt forced.

I couldn't stop thinking about Lily. The few seconds that her lips trembled before forming a thin, hard line that still looked strangely alluring. I liked it when she got angry enough to show some of the fire I sensed simmering beneath her sweet, good girl surface. I'd never liked a passive woman. Kim, problematic as she was, was proof of that. She'd burned bright as a torch when we first met as teenagers. She was burnt out now, and the years of living high on the child support she didn't use to support our child were coming to an end. I was afraid she was determined to go out with a bang.

"Hey, earth to Con." Julian snapped his fingers in front of my face.

I smacked his hand away. I could always tell what movie Julian was focused on by the lingo he used. Right now it must be the sequel to the sci fi blockbuster that came out last summer.

"Sorry, I'm distracted." I sketched out an explanation about Kim and the shit I was dealing with at work. And then, almost as an afterthought, I added, "And I've got Halley's sorority sister to deal with on top of it."

"Deal with?" Garrett repeated.

"Yeah," I said, then when they continued to stare blankly at me, I elaborated. "Halley made me pick her up from the airport the other day, and today I had to take her to lunch."

There was a beat, then Dominic said, seemingly for all of them, "That's rough, pal."

Julian snickered first, then the rest joined in. My irritation notched up. "I'm not a fucking babysitter."

"And she's not a baby," Landon said. Then he looked closer at me, spotting something the others had missed. Damn his intuition. It made him great at security and fucking obnoxious as a friend. "Or is that the problem?" he asked astutely.

The snickers became raised eyebrows.

"There's no problem," I said shortly, finishing my beer. "I'm just too busy to play tour guide right now."

"Has anyone seen this tourist?" Landon asked the group. "What does she look like?"

They shrugged. Garrett said, "I'll find her."

I had no doubt he could do it, too. He and Halley were connected on social media. I stayed away from all that shit minus the Instagram profile I had for The Walker Agency, but I imagined Lily had Snapchat or Tik Tok or whatever the hell Millennials were into these days. When Garrett pulled out his phone, I said, "Put that away, asshole. I don't want you stalking my daughter's friends."

"Then tell us what she looks like," he said, his thumb pausing over the screen.

An uncomfortable itch crept under my collar. The last thing I wanted to do was think about what Lily looked like, much less describe her. "She's blonde," I muttered.

"Of course she is," Dominic said, and the others laughed.

"What the fuck does that mean?" I demanded. Then I was treated to an uncomfortable recitation of my dating history. All of them were blondes.

"It's LA," I defended myself. "Everyone is blonde."

Garrett looked around theatrically at the table behind us. Just my luck, it was filled with brunettes.

"Fuck off," I said, giving up. "It doesn't matter what color her hair is. I'm not interested in her. She's a kid."

I could see them glancing at each other sideways, trying to figure out who had the balls to say it. Of course it was Landon, with his martial arts training and concealed weapon permit. "She's not a kid though," he said, scratching his chin. "She's older than Halley, right?"

"And Halley is a kid," I said through clenched teeth.

"Sure, she's a kid to us," Garrett stepped in. "But legally, I mean, she's twenty-one. How old is Lily?"

"Twenty-three." The syllables barely escaped through the tight clamp of my jaw.

Another long pause. Dominic stepped up this time. "When you were twenty-three, you had a four-year-old."

And I was pulling six figures. But that was different. I'd had to grow up fast when Kim came to me with that positive pregnancy test. I'd had to leave all the friends I'd had behind to do it because they were still fucking around in college when I was heating up bottles at three am and working seventeen-hour days. Me at twenty-three and Lily at twenty-three were a world apart.

It was too hard to explain though, so I just said, "It's different."

"Undoubtedly," Julian said smoothly. "But we're just saying–"

"Well don't," I cut him off. "It doesn't matter how old

she is. She's Halley's friend, so she's off limits. And that goes for all of you." I narrowed my eyes and moved my gaze to each of them in turn.

Garrett held up his hands innocently. Landon gave me a dead-on stare that told me he'd do whatever the hell he wanted. Julian shrugged like it didn't matter to him one way or another. Dominic looked at me a moment longer, like he was trying to see what I wasn't saying. I glared at him for an extra moment.

"Okay," he said finally. "She's off limits."

Each of them nodded, even Landon. The band of tension around my chest loosened slightly. I hadn't even realized that I had stiffened, but the irritation was still pulsing through me. I knew my friends would keep their word—they'd keep their hands off Lily.

Now I just had to make sure I could keep mine off, too.

8

LILY

The fire in my cheeks seemed to burn for the entire afternoon. Even Victoria, the brand development specialist in the desk nearest mine who had barely said good morning when I introduced myself, said something about it. She must not have been invited to lunch either, because she was sitting at her desk with a salad when I came in, a little dazed, a lot humiliated.

"Did you get a sunburn?" she asked as I sank numbly into my uncomfortable chair. I'd noticed earlier that everyone else had a fancy ergonomic chair. Now I could barely feel the hard, uncushioned seat or the strange curve of the back that seemed designed to puncture the spine.

"What?" I asked, trying to rest my arms on the armrests before I remembered it didn't have any. I crossed my arms over my chest instead. I could still feel my arms reaching out for Con, extending away from my body as if of their own volition.

He'd thought I was reaching out to hug him. That was humiliating, but not as humiliating as the truth. The truth was that I didn't know exactly why I'd reached for him. Maybe it was only to hug him goodbye—a reflex that had become ingrained in me after four years in the sorority. But God, I wasn't sure. It hadn't been a conscious action so much as an uncontrollable impulse to touch him. If he hadn't stopped me, who knows what I would have done next.

Likely, I'd have humiliated myself far worse.

"A sunburn. I think you got one. Your face is bright red," Victoria observed, pointing the tines of her fork at me and waggling them. "You need to start wearing sunscreen unless you want to look like a leather handbag by the time you're thirty."

Lily, this isn't a sorority. In the real world, you shake hands with someone to say goodbye instead of rubbing up against them.

Con thought I was a moronic, juvenile, child. That stung. But not as badly as him thinking that I was trying to rub up against him. Mostly because I was afraid that I was.

"It's not a sunburn," I finally managed to answer her. I wanted to put the backs of my hands to my cheeks to cool them, but Victoria was watching me too closely. I wished she'd go back to ignoring me the way she had all morning.

"Then what is it?" she asked bluntly, popping a bite of salad in her mouth and chewing intently, her dark gaze never wavering from my face.

I desperately wanted to confide in someone, but Victoria was the last person I'd trust with my secrets. I barely knew her, but I knew her type too well. She was interested in me right now because she sensed there was something of interest going on beneath this supposed sunburn. If I gave her an opening, she'd root around until she found something of value to bring back to the other women in the office. Then she'd try to trade my secrets for a lunch invitation, like they were social currency.

I said the first thing that came to mind. "Rosacea."

Her nose wrinkled. She pushed back her chair slightly, as if it was contagious. "Ew. Isn't there a cream for that?"

"Yes, but it's not working right now." I gave into the impulse to put the cool backs of my hands to my cheeks and smiled at her between them. It was my turn to root around. "Why didn't you go to lunch with the others?"

I knew why. It was because they hadn't asked her. Other than me, she was the newest to the office. This was clearly a hierarchical environment that factored in time served. It gave me a bad taste in my mouth, like I was going backward. I hadn't dealt with a clique like this since high school. Despite what people thought about sororities being exclusionary, ours really had been inclusive. I'd been cocooned by friendship since I was nineteen. I never thought I'd feel the overlording presence of a queen bee again at twenty-three.

Victoria's avid gaze flickered away as she chewed, swallowed, and speared another bite. "Someone has to stay here to watch the phones," she said unconvincingly. I felt a stab of pity at the pinched, unhappy expression on her face. At least I was only here for two months before I rotated to a new division. This was where Victoria was trying to make her career, and she didn't look much older than me.

"I'll stay next time," I said.

"I mean, yeah. That would be fair." She crunched down on her salad.

I rolled my eyes and shifted in my chair, trying to find a comfortable position. That would teach me to be nice.

Nice. That was all I was being earlier with Con. Friendly. It wasn't what he made it sound like. I felt my cheeks heat again, but luckily Victoria was too engrossed in her phone to notice. I heard his low, tense voice in my ear again, but along with the embarrassment, a thrill of excitement went through me at the idea. A small, distant voice reminded me that this was Halley's dad I was thinking about "rubbing up against," but that wasn't how I thought about him anymore.

My cheeks felt like they stayed warm throughout the rest of the afternoon. I'd forget about what happened with Con for a little while, but then something would happen that put me right back on the sidewalk. The sun at my back. My shadow stretching out to meet the tips of his fancy leather shoes. The way the rugged panes of his face shifted, first in surprise, then into something that I couldn't identify, and then settled into the hard mask. I wished he didn't wear those dark-framed sunglasses everywhere. If I could just see his eyes, maybe he wouldn't be such a mystery to me.

By the time I left at the end of my first day, I was exhausted. Dealing with the exclusionary politics of the brand development team would have been tiring enough, but the way Con had completely taken over my brain was another. Not just my brain. My body kept reacting to the idea of him, the fantasy of us. It didn't matter that the reality was that he'd pulled away like I was a leper, and that he was the most off-limits man in the world to me, even if he was interested. Which he definitely was not.

The strange, deliciously unsettling feeling in the pit of my stomach that told me he might be was just wishful thinking. A juvenile, sorority-girl fantasy. *Time to join the real world, Lily,* I lectured myself as I stepped out onto the street in the bright sunshine.

It was a beautiful evening. The sky was still bright blue, and the world felt awash in light and luxury. As I walked toward Halley's condo, it seemed like everywhere I looked, extraordinarily beautiful people were stepping into town cars that were ready to whisk them away to fancy restaurants or exciting parties. It seemed to me that these people were all living in an idealized version of the real world.

They weren't walking home alone, fantasizing about someone they could never have.

At the end of my second week, despite the beauty of the day and the place and the people, my heart grew heavier with every step I took. It took me most of the way back to Halley's condo to identify the feeling.

I was lonely.

Of course I was. Other than an occasional conversation with Victoria or a pleasant exchange with a nice guy at work named Devon, I spent most of my time alone. Once in a while I had lunch with Maureen, Con's EA who I'd gotten to know over the last few years because she was always available to help Halley and I when we were traveling and in a bind. But as much as I liked her, I was still alone most of the time.

I hadn't been lonely in—God, I couldn't remember. In college, I'd lived with no fewer than thirty girls. It was impossible to take a shower in complete privacy, without someone banging in to ask to borrow your clothes or to see if you wanted to grab coffee, much less get lonely. In high school, I'd had a few good friends I could always count on. I had to trace this sensation all the way back to early middle school—when my elementary school clique fell apart and I found myself adrift, unmoored, in the sea of puberty.

I'd felt awkward and hopeful and desperately alone, and it killed me to realize that was exactly how I felt now, a lifetime later.

Back in Halley's condo, I tried to ignore the feeling by completely unpacking and then going through each cabinet to get a sense of what I had to work with in the kitchen. The feeling kept pace though. I wanted—no, I needed to talk to someone. I called my mom, but she was at her book club. I called one of my close friends, but she was in class. It was just as well none of them was picking up though, because the person I really wanted to talk to was my best friend.

Halley.

As I stared down at the phone in my hand, undecided, it lit up. And of course it was her. We'd always been closer than sisters. Practically able to read each other's minds.

True to form, the first thing she said when I answered was, "You miss me, don't you?"

"Oh my God, you have no idea." I gave into the sweet rush of happiness her voice brought me. "I've had a day."

I poured myself another glass of the fancy dry white I'd found in the refrigerator and told her about the brand development team. Halley alternately laughed and groaned at my description of how cliquey they had been.

"I'm sorry, Lily. That's how LA is. I mean, you'll find nice people eventually, but you have to really scour the woodwork. They're not just going to pop out." There was a long pause, and I heard computer keys clacking. Halley was doing homework while we talked. I closed my eyes and leaned my elbows on the cool granite countertop of the bar, pretending I was sitting at the end of her bed with my own computer sitting on my crossed legs.

"What about guys?" Halley asked after a moment.

My eyes popped open. "What about them?"

It had been an off handed question, but something in my voice caught Halley's attention. "Oh," she said with a hint of glee. "There's a guy."

"There is not a guy," I corrected. It was true. There were a million guys in LA. None of them any more special than the other, as far as I was concerned.

"There's a guy," Halley said, distracted again. I heard keys clicking, then she came back, focused again. "Tell me about him."

With a sigh, I slid off the barstool and walked around the living room, then out onto the patio. Far below, I saw figures splashing in the pool. On one end, a woman in a lime green one-piece was swimming methodical laps. I watched her cut through the water like a tropical fish while I figured out what to say to Halley. I desperately wanted to unburden myself and tell her everything. Surely, I wasn't the first of her friends to think her dad was hot. Unless they'd all been blind.

Maybe if I could have done it with enough levity in my voice, I would have told her the truth. Disguised it in a joke, of course, but still, I might have been honest. But I couldn't. Instead, I took a sidestep away from the truth and said, "You know me too well. There is a guy. Maybe you know him—I ran into him at the pool yesterday."

And then I described everything I was feeling about Con and attached it to this mysterious tenant.

"I'm confused," Halley said. "Why would he think you're too immature for him?"

"Because he's older," I explained, still watching the woman in the lime green suit swim. "And I guess I came off kind of ditzy."

"Hmm," Halley said, unconvinced. "You don't really give off ditzy vibes. Did you say something dumb?"

I shook my head, then realized that I wasn't really sitting at the end of her bed and therefore she couldn't see me. "I don't think so, but you know, I talked about being in a sorority. You know how people can be about that."

"Sure," she said doubtfully. "But if that's the conclusion he leapt to, he seems like an ass."

"He might be," I admitted with a sigh, picturing Con's dark, impatient eyes when he met me at the airport. "But Halley, he's so good looking, it hardly matters."

Now she laughed. "You sound like me! Don't let LA get

in your head, Lily. If he's an ass, it doesn't matter how good looking he is, he isn't good enough for you."

"Sure, sure," I muttered. It was funny, I'd never been insecure before. Not since early middle school anyway. A couple of weeks in LA though, and I was full of self-doubt. I wasn't sure how much of that was the place and how much was the man. I'd had crushes before, but this felt different. Crushing. I desperately wanted Con to be sparing me even a tenth as much mental attention as I was spending on him.

"Seriously," Halley said again, but I could hear her keyboard clicking beneath her long, lacquered nails. "Don't waste your time on him."

"You're right," I said, resolve surging through me. I wasn't going to waste any more time thinking about someone I could never, ever have.

Halley was more important to me than her father ever could be.

9

CON

I avoided the Brand Development department like the plague for the next couple of weeks. It wasn't hard. I was busy as hell with the new crop of problems that had sprung up since I solved the others. When I first started in this business, I thought that a good agent got to the point where there were no fires actively burning. That if I worked hard enough or long enough, I could take a long, deep breath and not feel the jabbing pressure of unresolved issues. It took me a few years of working myself into the ground to realize that point never came. I could have worked every minute of every day for the rest of my life, and people would still be waiting longer than they wanted.

But I learned that the problem wasn't me—it was just that this was an impatient town filled with people who wanted to come first and foremost to every single person in their orbit. And try as I might to avoid it, narcissists made this world go round. It used to piss me off, but after two decades, I finally understood that it took a certain kind of person to think they could make it in this industry. If I only signed levelheaded, reasonable actors, my roster would whittle down to less than what my father had maintained. I had to take the big problems with the big payoffs, or *I* wouldn't make it in this industry. That had been hard when Halley lived at home, but now I had all the time in the world. I could spend every waking second putting out fires if I wanted to. And if doing so kept me from thinking certain, inappropriate thoughts, then that was just another benefit.

For the rest of August, I rolled up my metaphorical sleeves and got my hands dirty. I took a cutthroat approach to contract negotiations that kept me haggling long into the night, and I enjoyed it. I'd never been able to completely immerse myself like this because I'd had a daughter to take care of. As it turned out, I liked dropping off to sleep with millions of dollars running in circles around my brain. It wasn't about the money, really. I had more than enough for the rest of mine and Halley's life. It was the challenge.

Although on the rare morning when I didn't have a meeting or a problem to solve, the challenge was finding something to do other than think about how Lily was two floors below. I'd caught a glimpse of her here and there, her golden hair shining like a beacon as she walked through the lobby.

I never saw her with other members of the brand development team, and it made me wonder. I tried to keep my finger on the pulse of company culture, so I knew they weren't the most welcoming department. I considered calling Angelina Bangert, the head of it, but I knew that might be counterproductive. Angelina had made it clear she wanted to be more than colleagues a few years ago, and I'd rebuffed her.

Two weeks after my ill-fated encounter with Lily on the sidewalk, Landon and I met for lunch. He didn't have much time, so we went to a sandwich shop that was never crowded and sat under the striped awning in a table that faced the sidewalk, our backs to the windows of the shop. Landon glanced around a few times before he was satisfied that no one was in earshot and then said, "I don't have anything yet."

"Then why did you practically sweep the fucking table for bugs before we sat down?" I asked, exasperated. Landon's caution was legendary. It was why he was the best, but it was also aggravating as hell to be his friend sometimes. Even at the place we'd gone for happy hour every week for the last fifteen years, he liked to sit with his back to the wall and insisted we always have the same server.

Landon shrugged, unconcerned. His philosophy was that if you never let your guard down, you never slipped up. He bit into his sandwich and chewed, his eyes surveying the street all the while as if he was doing a threat assessment.

"She's got Hayes and Sons tailing you," he said after he swallowed. "Mid-level firm on its way down. You've probably noticed."

"I've definitely noticed," I said wryly. The car that had tailed me so conspicuously two weeks ago hadn't let up. Occasionally he drove a different vehicle, but it was practically a joke between us now. He waved hello in the morning, and I gave him the finger. Once I sent him a drink when I noticed him sitting across a restaurant I was eating dinner at, and he gave me a thumbs up when it arrived.

"Word is, she paid them a retainer, but they haven't seen a dime since," Landon said. "They're not exactly highly motivated right now."

"Good." We ate our sandwiches in companionable silence for a while. I was idly watching people walk by. Landon was studying them with narrow eyed intensity that caused some to look back uneasily.

Then he said, "Do you know her?"

I glanced up, expecting to see a client or a colleague, or

maybe even someone who wanted to be a client and recognized me. I didn't expect to see Lily staring at me. The sight of her was like an electric shock. My heart jumped, and the hair on the back of my arms stood up. Landon noticed, of course, and raised his eyebrows over his sunglasses. "I guess you do."

Lily had been walking toward us from the direction of the agency, but she must have stopped short when she saw me. Now that I was staring back at her, she started walking again. I could sense her reluctance in the way her hands knotted together even as she set her chin firmly.

"Hi," she said when she reached us. She glanced at me, then smiled at Landon politely.

Landon stood smoothly and held out his hand. "Landon Campbell."

"Lily Anderson." Her smile brightened as she shook his hand, and she tucked her shining blonde hair behind her ear. "I'm Halley's friend. Mr. Walker was kind enough to give me a job at his company for the next year."

Landon's cheek twitched, the only sign he gave that he was amused by anyone referring to me as *Mr. Walker.* "Con doesn't give anyone anything," he said. "You must have earned it."

"She graduated with a 4.2 GPA, and she got accepted to several top tier law schools," I said before Lily could respond. "I figured a year here would scare her away from entertainment law."

Lily looked at me, clearly surprised I'd bothered to look at the resume she'd sent when she thanked me for the internship. I hadn't at first. It was only in the past two weeks I'd opened her email again and looked at the attachment. It was clearly an undergraduate's resume, but it was impressive for what it was. She'd had leadership roles in her sorority, as she'd mentioned at lunch. She'd also attached her transcript, so I knew that her course load hadn't been a cakewalk.

"And don't call me Mr. Walker," I added, meeting her gaze for the first time since I'd snapped at her on the sidewalk two weeks ago. "It's Con."

"Or asshole," Landon said, surprising her into a laugh.

"I'll stick with Con," she said, her eyes still on mine. What could only be described as a frisson ran through me as I stared back at her. I was aware of Landon glancing back and forth between us, his bemusement morphing into comprehension, but I still couldn't look away.

Finally, the sound of the bell above the sandwich shop door tinkled as someone came out. Distracted, Lily glanced up. My eyes stayed on the curve of her cheek, the defined underline of her jaw, the glint of a diamond stud in her earlobe.

"I'd better go get my lunch," she said, breaking the spell.

I wrenched my gaze away before she could capture it again. My heart was beating unpleasantly fast, and low, throbbing irritation was simmering up. I didn't want to notice her glowing skin and golden hair. And I sure as hell didn't want Landon to see me noticing. I felt his gaze boring into the side of my head. When I didn't look back, he said to Lily, "I'll pull up a chair."

"Oh, no," she said hurriedly. "I have to get back for a meeting. It was nice meeting you, Landon. I'll see you back at the office, Con."

The bell tinkled again as she went inside. Landon waited until the door closed behind her, then raised his eyebrows expectantly at me.

"What?" I asked belligerently.

"That's what I'm asking you," he said. "Although my question is more like, what the hell are you thinking? Didn't you make us all swear a fucking blood oath not to touch this girl because she's *just a kid?*"

I shot him a killing look. "I'm not thinking anything. So whatever you *think* I'm thinking, keep it to your fucking self."

"That's great advice. Make sure you follow it since that's your daughter's best friend." Landon's voice was low and pleasant, but his tone carried an unmistakable warning.

I bristled, even though I knew it came from a good place. Landon had seen the way I looked at Lily. Knew what it meant. He was trying to keep me out of trouble, the same way Garrett tried to reign in his clients as their crisis manager. But this wasn't a crisis, and I didn't need to be managed.

"I know who she is," I snapped. "And even if she wasn't Halley's best friend, she's a Walker Agency employee. I don't fuck with employees as a rule."

"Good. Don't break it." Landon sat back, prepared to let it go.

But when Lily walked out again, holding the box with her sandwich, I couldn't help but follow her with my eyes all the way down the sidewalk until she crossed the street with quick, light steps and disappeared from view.

Landon sighed and shook his head. He didn't need to say anything. I knew.

I was in trouble.

10

LILY

For two weeks, I'd managed to stay out of Con's sight. I couldn't believe that after avoiding him so carefully at the office, I'd ended up walking right up to him at the sandwich shop. I'd specifically gone there because it was the cheapest place within walking distance. After seeing his lunch place of choice with its twenty-five-dollar side salads, I'd thought there was no way he'd be there. Just my luck, I was wrong.

My heart beat like a jackhammer as I walked back to the office, only slowing slightly when I was out of his sight. It was crazy, but I could have sworn I felt his eyes on my back the whole way. It made me both self-conscious and light-headed with a crazy sort of desire I'd never felt before.

I told myself over and over that it was crazy, that I couldn't keep thinking about Con that way. I just couldn't. But all day, thoughts of him intruded on whatever I was doing, wherever I went. And of course, Halley called when I was walking home. I told her the carefully edited version of what was happening with my mystery crush.

She blew out her breath in a noisy sigh. "Lily, have you forgotten everything I taught you?"

I racked my brain, trying to think of any nuggets of wisdom that might apply to wanting to crawl on top of her dad. "I think so," I said finally when none came to mind.

"If you want to get over someone—even if it's someone you never actually got under—you have to find someone else! Go find a new crush. Preferably someone who doesn't make you feel insane. Someone nice. You used to like them that way."

"And you told me they were boring," I reminded her.

"They were!" she laughed. "But boring beats jerk."

I thought about Con telling Julian my GPA with a strangely defensive note, like he was standing up for me. "He isn't *not* nice," I said.

"Hmm," she said, unimpressed. "I'm going to need you to do better than that if you want me to support this crush."

I winced. "It's not a crush, Halley. It's just—I don't know. Temporary insanity."

Before she got off the phone, she extracted a promise from me that I would go out this weekend. She threatened to call up her high school friends to drag me out to a club, but I told her I had a friend from work I could ask. I was thinking about Victoria, even though she was more of a neutral non-enemy than a friend. All we had in common was that we were both outcasts in Brand Development, but surely that was enough to grab a drink together after work. It wasn't like we were being invited to the team happy hour anyway.

* * *

The next day, Victoria seemed surprised when I asked her if she wanted to grab a drink after work on Friday. I tried not to roll my eyes when hers instinctively went to Angelina Bangert, the team lead and queen bee of the social group. Angelina was in her office, back ramrod straight, fingers flying across her keyboard. She was nodding, and we could see her cherry red lips moving. Either mouthing along with what she was typing, or talking to someone on the phone, we couldn't tell.

"I guess so," Victoria said slowly, her eyes coming back to mine. "Friday isn't really a day that people do things though."

I knew what she meant, and it made me want to roll my eyes again. If you were trying to break into the LA scene, you were more likely to see interesting people mid-week than on a weekend. And it seemed like everyone into this office wanted to break into the scene. "I figured you'd be busy earlier in the week," I said more generously than I would have thought possible. I must really be desperate to get out.

Victoria was pleased by my assumption that she was very busy on the more important nights of the week. "I suppose I could," she said. "Where do you want to go?"

I had no idea where there was to go, and I said so. Victoria sighed gustily. "Of course you don't. Let me talk to some of my friends, see what's happening on Friday. *If* there's anything happening."

I felt a surge of mild alarm. I didn't want to go to anything that was *happening*. I thought we'd go to a bar or restaurant nearby, take advantage of the happy hour, and I'd hopefully meet some nice guy to take my mind off Con. But on Wednesday, Victoria announced officiously, "I've figured out what we can do on Friday. There's an opening in WEHO. People should be there."

The way she emphasized the word *people* told me she didn't just mean anyone. I cringed inwardly. I didn't want to meet *people*. "Where's WEHO?" I asked.

"Haha," Victoria said drolly. "Make sure you dress up on Friday, okay?"

I called Halley later and found out that WEHO was an acronym for West Hollywood. "That's dumb," I complained, a prickle of embarrassment running down the back of my neck.

"Is it?" Halley laughed. "I never thought about it. It's like SOHO or TriBeCa in New York. Everyone knows what it means."

I didn't know what either of those things meant. "I'm from Ohio," I reminded her. "And we just say the whole names. It's not hard. Dayton. Columbus. Yellow Springs."

"Very good," Halley said politely.

"Thank you." I ignored the patronizing note in her voice in favor of frowning into my closet. "I have no idea what to wear."

We switched to FaceTime so Halley could inspect the contents of my closet. When she agreed that there was nothing suitable, she sent me to the guest room closet to retrieve some of her clothing.

"These are too small," I complained as I tried on various outfits, trying to find something that didn't feel like I was painting it on. I frowned at the phone that I'd propped up on the nightstand.

"They're not too small," Halley corrected, her voice sounding small and faraway. She glanced up from the paper she was writing. "That one is good. Wear that."

I looked in the mirror again. It was the best option so far. It was a black dress with thin straps that looked simple when it was hanging up, but the thin, rich fabric slicked down my body, accentuating my curves and setting off my blonde hair. Somehow it made my waist look smaller and my chest bigger. I still didn't look a thing like the models I saw everywhere, but I didn't look bad. I tugged at the scooped neckline.

"Stop it," Halley ordered.

I pulled my hands away and resisted the urge to tug down the hemline, too. "It's not too short?"

"It's short, not too short. And you're going to look like a nun next to some of the girls there, trust me." Halley was looking down again, and I could tell I was losing her attention. Then I heard a voice call out to her, "Ready for dinner?"

A pang went through me. I missed going to dinner with my friends. Sometimes it had been an amorphous mass of us descending on the dining hall and pulling tables together. Sometimes it was just two or three. Either way, it was better than eating alone on Halley's pink couch every night. And it was a million times better than forcing myself to go out with a girl I wasn't sure I liked and definitely didn't trust.

"I've got to go," Halley said, slamming shut the lid of her laptop. "Wear that with heels and heavy eye makeup. It's perfect. You'll look like an off-duty rock star."

* * *

On Friday, Victoria came home with me after work. When she saw where I lived, she looked at me with curiosity and new respect. "Your parents must be rich."

"It belongs to a friend," I said evasively.

It had taken me nearly a week to feel comfortable in my best friend's condo. Victoria made herself at home right away, walking through each room, running her hands over furniture, even opening my closet. She looked from the contents of it to the black dress I had hanging on the back of the door, an eyebrow cocked.

"One of these things is not like the other," she pronounced, tapping the dress lightly with a long, black, stiletto nail.

I knew what she meant, so I wasn't going to ask her to clarify. Of course, she took it upon herself to do so anyway.

"This is designer. Maybe even off the runway." Victoria almost cooed the words. She was looking at the dress like she wanted me to leave them alone together. Then her gaze narrowed at the clothes hanging in the closet. "This is like, Mossimo."

I couldn't argue that. Many of my clothes *were* from Target. I offered an awkward shrug instead, wondering again if I'd made a huge mistake when I made plans with her.

Means to an end, I reminded myself. I'd find some nice guy to take my mind off Con tonight, and then Victoria and I could go back to ignoring each other in the office until I rotated away from Brand Development. God, it couldn't come too soon.

Victoria wandered into the kitchen and opened the refrigerator. Her gaze went right to one of the bottles of white wine that looked so expensive. Without even asking, she pulled it out and rifled through the drawers until she found the wine opener and wine glasses. "All right then," she said approvingly. "Your taste is...eclectic, but I can work with this."

I decided it wasn't the time to tell her I normally drank Barefoot wine. I accepted the glass she poured me, and we retreated to opposite bathrooms to get ready. Nerves made it hard to apply the eye makeup Halley had suggested but finishing my first glass of wine helped. I went out and poured myself a second, then carried the bottle to the other bathroom to top off Victoria's glass. She was struggling to get herself into a red dress that fit like Spanx. I looked for a zipper, but there was none. I set down the bottle and helped unroll the bottom of the dress from where it had bunched up in a tight band around her ribs.

"Thanks," Victoria said breathlessly, pulling it the rest of the way down. It was longer than mine, going nearly to her knees, but it was so tight I could see the indentation of her belly button, the striations of her ribs, and the thin line of her underwear. She frowned, seeing it too, and before I knew it, she was shimmying out of them.

"That's better," she said, nodding at her reflection decisively.

"Are you sure you can walk in it?" I asked doubtfully.

"If Kim can, I can." Victoria tossed her long dark hair back determinedly. She didn't look like she was going out to have fun. More like she was heading into battle. It was on the tip of my tongue to say *we who are about to die salute you.* I swallowed the words back and returned to my bathroom to get ready. I had more confidence now, and I plunged into my make up bag with more zeal. I didn't know if it was the wine or the realization that I couldn't possibly look as absurd as Victoria, no matter how much eyeliner I put on. When I was done, I hardly recognized myself. I didn't know if I looked sexy and sultry or completely ridiculous, but it was too late to turn back now.

I pulled on a pair of my own black heels—Halley's were too high—and walked out into the living room where Victoria was opening a second bottle of wine.

"Hope that's all right," she said when I saw her, sounding like she didn't care one way or another. "You look..." her gaze narrowed as she took me in from head to toe. "Are those Mix No. 6?" she asked patronizingly when her eyes reached my shoes.

I glanced down at them. "I'm not sure. I got them from DSW."

"Of course you did." Victoria popped the cork and poured us both generous glasses of wine. "Well good job on the dress, okay?"

Strangely, her attitude only added to my confidence. She was wearing heeled sandals with gladiator-style straps that wound their way all the way up her calves to just below her knees, where she'd tied them off so tightly that they made white indentations in her skin and her calves bulged between them, looking almost quilted. The straps themselves were covered in small silver studs that made the shoes look like they should be classified as weapons. There was a line of matching studs on the back of the heel that reminded me of a brontosaurus. She'd covered her face in makeup that was two shades paler than her own skin, and strangest of all, she'd smeared the foundation over her eyebrows so at first glance, it looked like she didn't have any.

If she didn't think I looked good, well, that was all right with me.

When we got to the opening of what, confusingly, was a restaurant even though it was set up like a club for this special opening evening, I didn't even feel self-conscious. Anyone who looked at us would skip right over me and stare at her. That would leave me free to peruse the available men in peace. I didn't have much hope of finding a nice, normal guy in this crowd, but stranger things had happened.

And being with Victoria had other advantages. She seemed to know exactly what to do and where to go. She navigated us through the line quickly, got us up to the bar in minutes, and even managed to procure one of the small cocktail tables. Despite her outcast status at work, she seemed to know people here, and before long, she'd collected a group around us. I quickly got the vibe that these weren't people I'd necessarily become friends with. They all seemed to have a similar mentality to Victoria. Even when they were talking to you, their eyes searched past you for someone more interesting. They deigned to speak to me at all because, like Victoria, I worked at The Walker Agency. I quickly discovered that working there was a type of currency in this world. It got me onto the lowest rung of importance. I had a feeling that if they knew I was friends with Halley Walker, I'd climb halfway up in one leap. Instinctively, I knew I'd never let them find out. I didn't want these strange, beautiful social vampires to think I had anything they wanted.

For a while, it didn't matter that I didn't really like who I was with. The novelty of being out was enough. Then I treated it like a fascinating anthropological study in which I got to observe the mannerisms of social climbing society up close and personal. When even that got boring, I started to search for the man I'd come here for. Someone nice, who wasn't buying into this either. I spotted a few possibilities, but either they were attached to someone or just *something* was missing. I couldn't quite put my finger on what.

After two hours of this, my feet hurt, and I was two drinks in too deep. I wasn't drunk exactly, but I wasn't entirely steady. I hated that feeling.

"I'm going to get water," I told Victoria. She glanced at me without comprehension, her mouth still moving a mile a minute as she gossiped with one of the other girls. Without bothering to repeat myself, I slipped away. Even with the alcohol buzzing in my bloodstream, I was starting to feel a little down. I didn't want to be at this fancy opening with these fascinating people. I wanted to be in my old sorority house with my friends. And I didn't want to be looking for nice boys like the kind I'd fallen for in Ohio.

I wanted Con.

The alcohol loosened the tight clamp my brain had put

on the thought, and it sprung open so suddenly I didn't have a chance to stuff it back down. I wanted him, and it didn't matter that he was Halley's dad or my boss. The desire was completely independent from reason, rational, and reality.

And then suddenly, he was there.

11

CON

The last place I wanted to be was at the opening of a restaurant I'd never eat at surrounded by people I'd never eat with. But Garrett had to go because he was on babysitting duty for a high-profile client who was on his last chance, and somehow, he swindled me into coming with him.

The interior was unusually dim, a line of pink LEDs outlining the contours of the room and the length of the bar. When people walked, the floor tiles beneath their heels and Italian loafers lit up lurid yellow and lime green. It was tacky as hell, and I didn't exactly have caviar tastes. I'd go anywhere that had decent beer and a minimum of assholes.

But based on the tap selection and the affected bartenders, this place struck out on both counts. I ordered from Bam Bam, a bartender who moonlighted as a bit player on a reality TV show and got myself the best they had to offer. With a sadistic twist of vengeful satisfaction, I got Garrett the worst. He hardly looked at the pint glass I put in his hand, his gaze fixed intently on his troubled actor.

He took a drink, then shifted his gaze to mine, his mouth twisting. "What is this shit?"

"Bam Bam recommended it," I said, trying not to grin.

"Who?"

I jerked my thumb in the direction of the bar. Garrett scowled, but before he could say anything, we heard his actor raise his voice.

Garrett's eyes snapped back, and he absent mindedly went back to sipping the piss-flavored beer, not even seeming to notice the taste anymore. I watched, mildly entertained, as he intercepted his charge's numerous forays into trouble territory. At one point, we had to relocate into the back room where there weren't any barstools, just low-slung tables surrounded by squat velvet armchairs. Iron chandeliers were wrapped in pulsating string LED lights that reflected off the mirrored walls, giving the place a nightmarish quality.

"I feel like I'm in hell," I called to Garrett over the music.

"Maybe, but at least hell doesn't have barstools."

I didn't have to ask him to explain. Everyone knew that his actor had picked up a barstool with every intention of smashing it over a rival's head last month. The jackass hadn't succeeded, only because he hadn't realized how fucking heavy a barstool was. Rumor had it that he'd fired his personal trainer the next day and replaced him with a bodybuilder.

"He's getting big," I said to annoy Garrett. "He'll be able to lift the whole bar soon."

"Shut up," Garrett snapped, and then because he couldn't help himself, he went to the bar to assess its structural integrity, that shitty beer still in his hand.

Laughing to myself, I headed back to the first room. Bam Bam may have been an idiot, but at least this tap had something halfway decent. I had developed tunnel vision long ago. It was effective both in my work and in situations like this, when I didn't want to make eye contact with a single fucking person who might recognize me and waste the rest of my night, trying to airdrop me their headshots.

That's why I was practically at the bar before I realized that the blonde blur in my periphery wasn't some faceless stranger who would always remain nameless. It was Lily.

I was almost used to the fucked-up combo of unpleasant shock and lust that punched into my solar plexus every time I came across her unexpectedly. But it still pissed me off. Especially when the shock was edged out by a darker version of the lust when I saw what she was wearing. Gone were the gauzy skirts and structured blazers, the subtle allusions to the shapely form beneath. Now she was wearing a black dress that skimmed down her backside, caressing without hugging her curves, and fluttered to an abbreviated end just below her ass. Her long, tan legs were bare, and she was wearing incongruously sensible black heels that didn't do a damn thing to slow the rush of blood from my head to my groin.

"What do you recommend?" she was asking Bam Bam.

He flashed a smile that was somehow even brighter than the LEDs. "The Pineapple Fantasy IPA. I'm actually the brewologist who created it."

If I hadn't been so distracted by the sudden appearance of Lily, I might have snorted. Bam Bam was a brewologist like I was a fucking wizard. A team had created it, and then, desperate for even the slightest bit of buzz, let him attach his bullshit name to it. Now he was hawking it. It was the cycle of bullshit that made this town go round.

"That's really cool," Lily was saying sincerely, even as reluctance was puckering her forehead. "I guess I have to try it."

"The fuck you do," I said, stepping forward. Garrett could afford to spend twelve dollars on beer that tasted like it had been sieved from the waste basin of a pollution plant. Lily couldn't.

"If you like IPAs, the Lunar Eclipse is the only decent one," I said, scanning the rest of the titles.

Bam Bam tried to scowl at me, but halfway through, he recognized me. It happened sometimes, no matter how hard I tried to keep a low profile. His mouth froze in an expression of perplexed dislike. I could almost see the thoughts cycling between his few brain cells. *This guy is an asshole. This asshole is Con Walker.*

"Con," Lily gasped. "What are you doing here?"

What an excellent question. I kept my gaze focused straight ahead. I knew if I looked at her, those cornflower blue eyes would be wide, and her pink lips would be parted with surprise. And more than that, I didn't want to see how low the neckline of her dress dipped.

"Two Lunar Eclipses," I said to Bam Bam.

When he turned around to pull them, I felt the pressure of Lily's wide-eyed gaze more intensely. Reluctantly, I looked back at her. "What are *you* doing here?" I asked, returning her question unanswered.

"Victoria invited me." Lily nodded to a dark-haired woman I recognized from Brand Development. So she was making friends. That was good, although I didn't like the looks of this one. She had that deadly combination of ruthlessness and hunger that I'd seen propel people both to the top of the world and into an abyss. Their sheer determination violated the natural order of gravity, and if you stood too close, there was no telling whether they'd bring you up with them or step on you to get there.

I hadn't realized I was staring at Victoria, my eyes slightly narrowed, until I felt Lily's hand on my arm. Again, that combination of shock and lust. This time though, it wasn't unpleasant. Still, I rolled my shoulders back, dislodging the gentle pressure of her fingers.

"I said, what are *you* doing here?" Lily repeated.

Bam Bam set our pint glasses in front of us. I paid for our drinks, ignoring Lily's gentle insistence that she would pay for hers.

"Thanks, man," Bam Bam said, his smooth affectation slipping when he saw the size of the tip I'd left. I heard a hint of the Midwest in his uncloaked syllables.

"It comes with a condition," I said. "If that guy—" I pointed across the bar to where he could see Garrett standing at the edge of the interior room "—orders another drink from you, tell him you *only* have Pineapple Fantasy left, okay?"

"Uh, sure," Bam Bam said uneasily, but I was already turning away.

I wasn't surprised when Lily followed me. I'd never answered her question after all. But it would have been easier if she hadn't. Not better. But fucking easier.

When we reached Garrett, I introduced them.

"Hi Lily," he said, still distracted by his problem actor, who was leaning so close to another actor that they were either about to start kissing or swinging. "I've heard a lot about you."

"You have?" she asked, surprised. She looked at me.

"I told him you were Halley's friend and that you were here for a job," I said levelly. "I'm not sure what Garrett's definition of *a lot* is."

"Not from him," Garrett said, finally turning his full attention to us. A hint of a smirk played at the corners of his mouth. "You've met another friend of ours."

Fucking Landon, of course. He'd sensed how I felt about Lily.

"Landon had a lot to say about me?" Lily said, clearly confused. "I only met him for a minute."

"He said you made an impression."

To anyone else, Garrett's expression might have looked sincere. I saw the malice dancing in his eyes though. He was going to get me back for making him drink twelve ounces of monkey spit, and he was going to laugh his ass off about it later with Landon. I felt the tendons in my shoulders tighten. Maybe his client wasn't the only one who would be throwing barstools tonight.

"I need to talk to you for a second," I said to Garrett, trying to keep my voice level. Lily's eyes widened again. Even Garrett looked surprised. He looked back at his actor, who at least for the moment, seemed reasonably docile.

"It'll only take a second," I said, baring my teeth in what I hoped Lily interpreted as a friendly grin. "It's about a work thing."

"Sure," Garrett said, not fooled. "Lily, you see that guy in the orange shirt over there on the leather settee?"

She nodded.

"If he tries to pick up that settee, or *any* of the furniture in here, I need you to get my attention right away, okay?"

Lily looked concerned.

"It'll only take a second," I repeated. I led Garrett over to a corner a few feet away and dropped my nice guy act. "Don't say another fucking word to Lily," I ordered, my voice low and deadly.

Garrett raised his eyebrows. "Ever? That's going to make the rest of the night pretty fucking awkward if you ask me."

"You know what I mean."

Over his shoulder, I saw Lily look over at us. She was mouthing something, but I couldn't figure out what.

"I don't know what Landon told you, but it's not fucking true," I continued.

"So you don't want to—"

I cut Garrett off with a hard look. Then, behind him, I saw Lily smile reflexively as someone approached her.

"It doesn't matter what I want. She's Halley's friend."

"But you do want to." Garrett finally finished his drink, wincing as he swallowed the dregs.

Before I could bite his head off, I caught an orange blur in my periphery. It was Garrett's has-been, leaning in on Lily like he had a broken leg and she was a set of crutches. She looked surprised to have his arm around her, like she wasn't quite sure how it had happened. But in true small-town-girl style, she still had a strained smile on her face. Halley would have decked the asshole and rammed a heel into his insole by now.

"Garrett," I said, my voice a growl.

"Keep telling yourself that then," he said, throwing his hands up. "See if I fucking care."

"Garrett," I repeated, stepping around him. I had it in mind to tell him to get his client under control, but my body wasn't willing to wait. My fists bunched up, the tension running all the way up the length of my arms, into my shoulders. I felt spring loaded as I moved toward Lily and the jerk wad who had his forehead leaning against her temple. He was whispering, and she was wincing. Likely at the smell of his breath, but maybe by what he was saying.

The idea of him talking to her like she was one of those sad, groupie girls who clung to anyone who was even halfway famous infuriated me, taking me from a level seven to a level ten so quickly I didn't process the escalation. I just reached out. My hand clamped down on his shoulder, fingers digging in like a bear trap. My other arm was cocked back, seemingly of its own accord.

"Con!" Lily gasped as I jerked the asshole away and angled myself between them.

"Con!" Garrett yelled in unison with her, finally realizing what was happening. Both he and Lily grabbed me before I could do anything else. He had me by the crook of the elbow, she was holding the tense arm that was still holding onto the other man. I had her worried face on one side and Garrett's concerned one on the other, but I had tunnel vision. All I could see was the asshole in front of me. His eyes were bleary, and he had a dopey smile on his face.

"No harm done, no harm done," he kept saying, trying to raise both his hands up, palms out. "I didn't know she was yours."

Offended, Lily started to explain to him that women weren't property, but I didn't want to muddy the waters. Guys like this needed things to be black and white.

"Well she fucking is," I said. "And if you ever touch her again, I'll rearrange your face so badly you'll need new headshots."

"And you really can't afford them right now," Garrett said quietly. "So come on, man. Let's get you home, all right?"

"No harm done," the guy repeated as Garrett led him off. "I didn't know. No harm done."

I watched him go, half hoping he'd make a break for it so I'd have a reason to deck him and release the tension that was immobilizing my body. And also so that I didn't have to look back at Lily, whose gaze was a blue beam in my periphery. When Garrett and his actor disappeared into the throng, I had no choice.

As I expected, her eyes were filled with confusion, and there was a question on her lips.

"I'm taking you home," I said roughly, finishing my beer in one quick gulp and slamming the pint glass down on the table. Fuck, if Garrett and Lily hadn't stopped me, I'd have smashed it into the asshole's face. Half of me couldn't believe I'd lost control like that. The other part of me still wasn't sure I'd regained it.

Lily arched one golden brow and said acidly, "As I was explaining to the other guy, women aren't property. I'll go home when I *feel* like going home." She started to turn away.

Frustrated, I grabbed her arm and pulled her back around, careful to keep my grip loose. She could pull away if she wanted. But she came willingly, even if there was blue fire in her eyes now.

"Lily, I'm leaving because I don't want to spend another second surrounded by assholes like the one I just pulled off you. And you're going with me because there's no way in hell I'm leaving you here alone."

When I'd pulled her around, I'd unconsciously pulled her up against me. I could feel her chest rising and falling in quick, tremorous bursts, like she was angry. Or excited. Her gaze had fallen to the hollow of my throat, and the pressure of it felt like it was strangling me. I should let her go. I had to let her go. Even if it meant she refused to leave, and I had to stay in this fucking bar all night to make sure no one else bothered her. I couldn't keep holding onto her like this.

Finally, she tipped her head back and looked up into my face, but the pressure in my chest didn't ease. "I don't want you to leave me here alone," she said quietly.

I wanted to pretend like I didn't know what she was saying, but I couldn't. Blame it on the beer or the adrenaline or the fucking dress she was wearing, I couldn't keep lying to myself, much less her.

I had to have her.

12

LILY

His eyes darkened, his face dipped lower, so close that I could feel the rasp of his breath. His head blotted out the too-bright lights. I couldn't hear the beat of the music anymore, but I could feel it. Rhythmic, pulsating. My heart matched its tempo as anticipation rose. When his mouth came down on mine, foreboding flashed through my mind. This was *wrong*. Halley would never forgive me. But as his strong arm encircled my waist, pulling me the rest of the way against him, my mind dissolved. Sensation took the place of reason because Con was kissing me. Really kissing me, his devilishly expert tongue parting my lips. Desire deepened in my belly and dampened the apex of my thighs. My legs were shaking, but it didn't matter because he was holding me against his hard chest so tightly, I was hardly supporting myself.

I'd never been kissed like this. In a strange, disjointed manner, the faces of the boys I'd loved ran across the projector of my half-closed lids. All of their faces were blurry, even that of my most recent ex, the one I thought maybe I would get back together with when we were at the same law school. And then they were gone, dissolving like my trepidation as Con deepened the kiss, his tongue tangling demandingly with mine.

Instinctively, my fingers had curled in the front of his shirt. Now I wound my arms around his neck, pressing myself full against him. It was as though the rich, filmy fabric of the dress didn't exist. I could feel every muscle, hard against me. The ridge of his pectorals, the hard pane of his stomach, the bulge of his belt buckle, and then a larger, harder bulge beneath, pressing into my hip.

The parade of boys I'd loved before receded even further into the past. I'd never once felt like this with any of them, like I wanted to keep going. I wasn't completely innocent, but somehow, I'd known that whatever I felt for them wasn't enough. This was what I had been waiting for.

Then, suddenly, there was an explosion of light. Con jerked back, his hands flying up to grip my arms, still wrapped around his neck. His disturbingly dark eyes were blacker than ever as they scanned the area, looking for the source of the bright flash. He looked dazed and wary, like a dangerous animal that had just been jolted out of hibernation.

A bouncer separated himself from the queue at the front door, his large shoulders cutting through the crowd as he made his way toward us. For a horrible, confusing moment, I thought we were his destination. He was going to throw us out. Public indecency. A dozen other hysterically puritanical fears chased their way through my mind before I realized where he was really going. Toward two girls who were so clearly from out of town that even I could peg them as tourists. They had a selfie-stick raised, and they were grinning up at it, trying to discreetly get a celebrity I vaguely recognized in the shot. But again, their flash went off. They exploded in laughter.

"No pictures," the bouncer said when he reached them.

One of them began to argue. I looked back at Con, hoping to find his smoldering gaze on mine, ready to reignite the interrupted kiss. He was looking at me, but not the way I'd hoped. Something had fractured in his gaze, and I saw self-recrimination mixed in with the lust. His fingers were tense, bracketed around my forearms. Even as I swayed toward him again, he pulled my arms down from around his neck.

Disappointment and confusion swirled in my chest. There was still heat in his eyes, but a wall had gone up.

"What's wrong?" I asked, my voice breathless.

Con shook his head, then nodded in the direction of the door. Letting go of my arms, he put a hand to the small of my back and firmly guided me through the crowd, out into the warm night.

"I should say goodbye." I looked over my shoulder for Victoria, but she was nowhere to be seen. Con shook his head when I started to go back.

"No." He bit off the word. "Let's go."

A thrill ran through me, but the look on his face quickly doused any hope I had that the reason he wanted to leave was to resume what we'd started. We started walking back toward my—Halley's—condo. His face was grim in the glow of the streetlamps. He kept his hands shoved in his pockets. I had to take two steps to his every one to keep up with him.

We walked in ominous silence for a few minutes, until my heel twisted beneath me, and I let out a sharp cry.

Con turned in time to see me grab the nearest light post. I reached down and rubbed my ankle. It had been a quick pain, already fading. "Are you okay?" he asked, but his voice was devoid of any emotion. His leg jangled impatiently, like he wanted to keep walking.

"Go on," I said peevishly. "You don't have to wait for me."

"Of course I have to wait for you," he said in the same dispassionate way. "I'm walking you home."

I straightened, putting my weight back on my ankle without bothering to test whether it was ready to take it. I *wouldn't* be weak around him. "I didn't ask you to walk me home," I snapped. "Maybe I'm not even ready to *go* home."

I'd have happily gone home if he was coming with me, but I didn't even have to ask. Every muscle in his body seemed tensed to get as far away from me as possible. His eyes though—they were still drinking me in.

Con was staring at my ankle. Now his gaze traveled slowly up the length of my leg. I felt it like a laser beam. Heat bloomed in my cheeks when he reached my curve of my breasts and lingered before lifting his gaze to the hollow of my throat. He must have been able to see my heart pounding in it. Finally, he reached my eyes.

"You're going home, Lily," he said quietly. "And you're getting in bed alone, like a good girl."

"Maybe I don't want to be a good girl." I meant for my voice to sound defiant, but somehow it just came out sounding small. Pleading. I barely recognized it.

An unhappy smile jerked the edge of his mouth. "It doesn't matter what you want."

He was saying it to me, but something about his tone made me think he'd been saying it to himself, too. Maybe over and over again, the same way I had. Hope blossomed in my chest. "What do *you* want?" I asked, my heart pounding at my nerve. I was seconds away from throwing myself at him.

Con's dark eyes flashed, then shifted in the direction of the tall white apartment building that rose up from the opposite side of the avenue. "It doesn't matter what I want either. Neither of us can have it."

Before I could think better of it, I reached for his arm. "Why not?"

He moved his arm out of my reach so smoothly that I grasped only air, but before my mind could even process what had happened, he was pulling me against him again and stepping backward until we were both in the shadowy alcove of a closed storefront. My body melted against his, and the relief of being against him made my knees weak. It wasn't over, he was going to kiss me again. We were going to go upstairs together, and—

But no. His face was not coming closer to mine. His jaw was hard, and his voice unyielding. "You're practically a kid. I'm supposed to be looking out for you, not thinking about doing things to you that I'd kill a man for doing to Halley." His voice was harsh with self-revulsion.

"But I'm not a kid." I reached up to skim my fingers along his iron jawline. "And I'm not your daughter. It's okay to--"

He squeezed me more tightly, cutting me off. His grip was painful now, but I still didn't want to pull away. Anything was better than the cold desolation hovering beyond the boundary of our interlocked bodies. This close, I could feel his heart pounding against his chest like an anvil. He lowered his head so that his mouth was at my ear. "There's nothing okay about what I'm thinking, Lily. And I'm not going to let it happen."

"Why not?" I whispered breathlessly. "No one would ever have to know."

My own words shocked me. Not only did I want to give myself to him, and only him, but I was willing to do it without even the guise of respectability. I, who had never even kissed someone before a second date, was pushing up against him, practically begging him to take me on a public street.

And he wanted to. Even as we were both trying to think of Halley first, the immediacy of our connection to her was fading. He was considering it. His grip was still punishing, but his fingers were tangling in the ends of my long hair now. His breathing was changing. He was painfully hard against me, his eyes an unfathomable shade of black.

I tilted my head back, prey offering her throat to a wolf.

Hoping he would bite.

13

CON

She was pliant in my arms, breath quivering. For once, her eyes weren't wide with surprise, but rather hooded and waiting. I could have her right there, and we both knew it. I flexed my fingers experimentally, imagining pushing her up against the stucco side of the wall and shoving that flimsy black fabric up around her waist. I'd lift her up, cover her mouth with one hand, and plow into her.

I saw it all.

Including what came after.

Disgusted with myself, I shoved her away before I could make the fantasy a reality. "Stay away from me, Lily," I growled, staying in the shadows even as she stumbled back out into the streetlamps. "Or I'll send you back to Ohio where you belong."

Her gaze narrowed, glittered. Her mouth, swollen from my bruising kiss earlier in the club, dropped open at the viciousness in my voice. She started to say something, but she must have thought better of it because suddenly she was turning away, practically running down the street. I watched, hands curled into fists, as she crossed the street and hurried to the front entrance of the condo building. She looked back when she reached the light spilling out from the lobby, one hand on the door. She couldn't see me still standing in the shadows, but she knew I was there. Watching her.

It took every bit of self-control I'd built up over the years not to go after her. To step even further back into the shadows and wait for her to go inside.

When she finally did, I began walking to my car. Fury and frustrated lust surged through me. It had been a narrow escape or a colossal mistake, or both. If it had been a mistake, I wanted to go back and see it through. Really fuck things up. Why not if I was going to feel like shit about it anyway? But a very, very small part of me retained a shred of sanity. Remembered that Lily wasn't just off limits because she was an employee in my agency, she was Halley's best friend. Fucking her would fuck me in the end. Between the Me Too movement and my daughter, I'd lose everything I'd worked for if this came out.

I got a chill under my collar, realizing how easily it could have come out. Thank God for those girls in the bar. If their camera flash hadn't jolted me out of my stupor, God only knew what I would have done to Lily in a public place. With another Walker Agency employee in the building. A sour pool formed in my gut, thinking about it. There was still a chance Victoria had seen us. If she had, she'd tell all of Brand Development. It would spread like a virus through the agency. If that was the case, by Monday, my executive assistant would have the unwelcome job of telling me about the rumor.

I'd find out soon enough.

I didn't sleep that night, or the next two for that matter. Every time I closed my eyes, I saw Lily's face again. Felt her in my arms. Her body curving into mine, her lips parting willingly beneath mine. I didn't know if it was better or worse knowing that if I'd said the word, I could have her entire body beneath mine.

On the third night, I did something I thought I'd never do. I logged in to The Walker Agency Instagram account, went to Halley's page, and found Lily's account. It was private, but I could see her profile picture. She was sitting on what I recognized as the east lawn of her college campus, leaning back on her arms, her legs bare in denim cut offs so short I could see the curve of her ass. She was smiling wide, her sunglasses pushed up on top of her head, eyes glowing up at the photographer.

A visceral desire to be the one standing over Lily grabbed me by the balls. Not in some wide-open field though. I wanted her in my bed, leaning back on her arms, smiling up at me as I stood over her. I'd push her knees apart, yank those denim shorts off her hips, down the length of her legs, over her ankles.

I leaned back in my chair and unzipped my fly. It had been a long ass time since I'd had to take care of myself, but there was no other option right now. I couldn't have Lily, and I didn't want a substitute. I stared at her picture, imagining it was her hands with the seashell pink nails wrapped around my shaft, jerking slowly up and down. Imagining how her lips would feel, taking their place, her blue eyes still wide and gazing up into mine.

I had to move to the shower for that image. The hot spray pounded down on my shoulders as I braced myself against the wall with one hand and finished myself off with the other. Lily's face imprinted against the back of my closed eyelids. In my imagination, I took her every way there was, and she begged me for more.

It was a long time before I got to sleep that night.

When the sky outside began to lighten on Monday morning, going from deep indigo to a foggy blue gray over the course of an hour, I felt like shit. My head was pounding from lack of sleep, and I was physically tired as though I had been chasing Lily around all night on foot, not just in my mind. I took another shower–cold this time–both to wake up and to drive out the lingering desire that tugged at my groin when I thought about her. It woke me up, but it did nothing to drive her out. Or improve my mood.

I went by Landon's office on my way to work to hear the latest with Kim. The PI she had tailing me was nowhere to be seen. I didn't know if it was because she'd given up or if she'd hired someone more discreet. I hoped it was the former.

"Looks like she's still retaining them," Landon said when I mentioned it. "And she even paid them some of what she owes them."

"But not all?"

He shook his head, and I breathed out a sigh of relief. The PI hadn't been around last night to see me with Lily, I was sure of it. If he had been, he'd have rolled down the window to congratulate me. He'd have snapped a picture with a blinding flash, and then laughed about it.

Landon studied me over his computer monitor. "You have something to hide all of a sudden?"

His voice was carefully neutral, but I knew what he was implying. "I'm not fucking the girl, if that's what you're asking," I said flatly.

"It was," Landon said. "And good. Keep it that way. The last thing you want is for Kim to get a picture of your dick in your daughter's best friend. She'll own you."

I pinched the bridge of my nose, digging my thumb and forefinger deep into my painfully dry tear ducts. "Eight more months and I'll be done with her."

"Financially, yes," Landon agreed cautiously.

"I'm going to throw a party. A fucking funeral."

The corners of Landon's mouth tugged into a faint smile. "She won't actually be dead though, pal. You'll still see her at Halley's graduation. Her wedding. You two will share grandkids. Remember that before you dance on her grave."

My anticipation soured. I'd known abstractly that Kim would always be in my life, but I hadn't thought about the details. I selfishly wished, not for the first time, that she had been a shitty mother instead of just a subpar one. One who would have taken a lump sum and swanned off to Bora Bora, never to think of her daughter again. The trouble was, Kim was just good enough a mother that Halley loved her, and so I was chained to her for the rest of my life. "You've got to give me something to bury her with at least," I said to Landon. "Who is she fucking, and who is she screwing?"

Landon ran through what his PI had gotten on her. It was nothing that surprised me. She was in a relationship with an investment banker, and she was suing a resort wear company that had promised her a bonus every time she posted a picture in their clothing that got over a thousand likes.

"What is she, a fucking influencer now?" I asked in disbelief. "Isn't she too old?"

"Thirty-nine is the new nineteen," Landon said, startling a laugh out of me.

"That's the company's tagline for her campaign," he said dryly, turning his monitor so I could see the promo. I glanced, disinterested. Kim looked beautiful as always, if airbrushed within an inch of her life. I was grateful Halley had taken after my side of the family though. It made it easier to forget her mother existed. At least, when I wasn't having to pay a PI to keep her money grubbing hands at bay.

"If she's getting brand endorsements and investment bankers, what does she want with me?" I asked, glancing at the name of the resort wear company. They were a mid-level company on the rise. I imagined they paid their influencers decently.

"You know Kim. She has expensive taste. And her investment banker isn't going to buy the cow. Not when he's getting milk from several other younger cows about town."

I rolled my eyes upward. "Please tell me she hasn't introduced this asshole to Halley as her future stepfather."

Landon turned the monitor again, and I saw a picture of Kim, Halley, and a slick-looking guy in a Saville Row suit walking out of a restaurant. He looked young and smooth and cocky as all hell. I hated him on sight.

My lip curled. "How old is he?"

Landon's dark eyebrows rose incrementally. "Older than Lily and richer than you."

"Fuck you." Frustrated, I stood up and walked to the window. "I don't give a shit who Kim is fucking or how much money he has. It'll never be enough for her. I need something to hold over her."

"I'm trying."

"Not something you create," I warned.

In the window, I saw his blurred, watery reflection shake its head. "No. I know the rules."

I cracked my knuckles, wishing Landon had a punching bag in his office. "You think there is something?"

There was a long pause. I didn't turn around to see if he'd heard me. When it came to sensitive information, Landon always chose his words carefully, placing each one in front of the other like a tightrope walker on a highwire. "I don't know," he said finally. "Used to be that Kim was always good for a few dark secrets. Nothing is coming out of the shadows now though. If there's nothing there, are you sure..."

I shook my head, and he didn't bother to finish the

sentence. If Kim had legitimately fucked up, which she usually did, I'd use it in mercilessly. But I couldn't risk setting her up. If Halley ever found out, she'd never forgive me.

And the list of unforgivable things that I was considering was long enough already.

14

LILY

At first, I had been too overwhelmed to process what Con had said. It was only when I was safely back in the condo that his words came back to me.

Stay away from me, Lily. Or I'll send you back to Ohio where you belong.

He'd send me back, would he? I grabbed my suitcase out from under the bed and unzipped it with jerky movements, shame and anger coursing through me. I wouldn't let him play puppet master with my life, jerking my strings depending on his mood. This way when he felt benevolent, that way when he felt malevolent. Generous and spiteful in turns. I tore Halley's dress over my head and pulled on a pair of jeans and a t-shirt. Then I began flaying the rest of my clothing from the hangers, tossing them in the yawning mouth of my knock off Samsonite that, like my clothes, came from Target.

But even before I was halfway through, I changed my mind. Con's words, bitter as they had been, were already losing their sting as I remembered the look on his face. Set in stone to hide the need, but it still burned in his eyes. He'd curled his fingers into fists, but I could still remember how they'd felt tangled in the ends of my hair. The wide expanse of his palm wrapping around the back of my head while he kissed me so desperately I nearly bent backward.

He wouldn't send me back to Ohio. He couldn't. Even if he took the job away, and his daughter's condo, he didn't own the city and he didn't own me. He couldn't order me out of LA, and as long as I was here, I had a chance. I sat down on the edge of the bed, determination and pride replacing the shame and anger. Con wanted me, no matter how hard he tried to deny it. And I wanted him. If I had learned anything in life, it was how to work for what I wanted. I wasn't like Halley—no one would ever hand it to me on a silver platter.

Slowly, I rehung my shirts and dresses, trying to formulate a plan. Con had told me to keep away from him because he knew what would happen if I didn't. All I had to do was the opposite. I had to be in his way at every turn. And I knew just how to manage it.

It was one am before I turned out all the lights and crawled between the silky sheets. The city lights still burned against the underside of the clouds, and the night sky outside my window was ominously red. It felt like a warning. If I stopped now, I could protect myself.

I rolled away from the window determinedly. I had played it safe long enough.

I dreamed about Con all night, what would have happened if he hadn't pushed me away. What still might happen if I managed to wear down his resistance. Over the weekend, I saw Victoria on Sunday morning for brunch—I paid for both of us as an apology for disappearing on her. It was a small price to pay to answer the question of whether she'd seen me and Con. She hadn't. She looked disinterested when I said I'd run into an old friend, and she spent most of the time telling me in exhausting detail about each and every person we'd met. Then she moved onto the people who hadn't been there, including the names of several D-list celebrities and socialites that I'd vaguely heard of.

Then, unexpectedly, she mentioned Halley. I had fallen into a habit of nodding mechanically, but at the familiar name, my eyes jerked to hers in surprise.

"Halley *Walker*," she said significantly. "As in, Con Walker's daughter. She's in her senior year of college on the East Coast."

I knew all that, even as I made a surprised, impressed face. But why had she come up? How was she connected to the group Victoria had introduced me to? And had any of them seen me kissing her father?

As Victoria went on, I relaxed. Apparently, Halley had dated one of the guys in high school, and he was still name dropping her. By extension, Victoria was now name dropping her.

"Do you know her?" I asked casually. It was genuinely impossible to tell by what she was saying. Victoria referred to Halley familiarly, but I couldn't figure out if there was a direct connection.

"Oh, sure," Victoria said as though it was no big deal. Her eyes slid to the side though, and I sensed she was lying. "You'll probably meet her, if you keep hanging out with us."

I tried to look impressed again, but what I mostly felt was pity. Did Victoria have any real friends? Was there such a thing in a place like this? No wonder Halley had flown across the country to go to college.

When we parted ways, I was free to begin phase one of my plan. I borrowed Halley's car for the first time and drove to a fancy lingerie store I'd found online. It had shopkeepers who actually came out from around the counter and helped you. An intimidatingly beautiful woman stripped me down and took my measurements, then guided me to the sexiest, flimsiest, most expensive garments I'd ever seen. If I'd seen the price tags before I saw myself in the three-way mirror, I might have refused to try them on. Unfortunately for my bank account, I didn't.

It was more money than I'd ever spent on lingerie—more than I'd ever spent on *any* clothing, including my prom dress. I didn't hesitate though. Right now, I was riding high on our kiss and the memory of Con's hands on my body. He could puncture that confidence though. A dismissive look, a patronizing word, and I might deflate. I'd need the bolster of knowing that what I was wearing underneath my clothes could bring him to his knees.

Would bring him to his knees, eventually.

While I was breaking in my credit card, I bought more clothes for work, too. Being surrounded by designer wear was starting to make me feel insecure in my college-girl-playing-dress-up outfits. I needed Con to see me as the woman I was and not the college student I'd been.

On Sunday night, I dreamed of him for the third night in a row. When I woke up on Monday morning, I had a strange feeling of satisfaction, as though I'd already broken down his resistance. It took me a few moments to realize why—in my dream, I had. We'd been alone in his office, and he'd pressed me back against the glass that separated his desk from the reception area. In my head, I'd kept worrying that Maureen would walk in and catch us. Not because I would be embarrassed, but because he would stop. And I never wanted him to stop.

I'd never much believed in prophecies and premonitions, but now I fervently hoped that both were real, and that I was inextricably binding him to me with the power of my incessant, obsessive thoughts. Today was the day I enacted phase two of the plan.

I put on one of my new outfits. Black pants that looked deceptively simple, but they hugged every curve and made my legs look a mile long, especially paired with my new heels. A blue, scoop-necked blouse that almost would have been too casual but for how perfectly it was cut and the richness of the silky fabric. The color made my eyes pop and my hair glow.

I felt a buzzy high as I walked to work. There were nerves lurking beneath, but I tamped them down. When I got to the building, instead of going straight to the Brand Development department, I went to the executive floor. I was relieved to see Con's office empty. I knew he generally had a Monday morning meeting outside the building, and I needed to talk to his executive assistant alone

Maureen pulled an apologetic face when I approached. "He's not in, Lily. Is there something you need?"

"No, I actually wanted to talk to you." I leaned against the side of her desk, glad that Con had such a warm EA. Prior to working here, I actually had more interaction with her than I had him. She was always who Halley called when we got in a jam while traveling. She'd wired us more funds, sent out repair men, geolocated gas stations, and over the summer, she'd even found us a doctor in Croatia when our friend sprained her ankle. Halley said that she was her dad's right hand.

I also thought she needed help. She was almost eight months pregnant, and I knew from eating lunch with her a few times that she was worried about going out on maternity leave. She hadn't liked any of the temps who had interviewed.

"You want to talk to me? What about?" Maureen asked, surprised. She could tell by my face it wasn't just a lunch invitation.

"I want to be your temp." I tried to keep excitement

from leaping into my voice. This was the most important part of my plan, and it was so perfect in my mind. What better way to put myself in Con's way, not just now and then when I could manage it, but every single day. I just needed Maureen to agree. "My time with Brand Development is up soon. I can move up here and start shadowing you. That will give us like, what, two weeks to get me up to speed?"

Maureen was eying me doubtfully, her mouth down-turned like a cat. "Lily, that's so sweet. But Con needs a professional. You just don't have enough experience, and two weeks isn't *nearly* enough time."

I'd thought she might say this. I had a backup plan. "Okay, then what if I'm the assistant to the temp EA," I said gamely. "I don't have certifications and experience, but I know Con and the company better than an outsider."

"It does seem like a two-person job sometimes," Maureen murmured. Her doubt was becoming speculation. She was wondering if it might just work.

"I worked the front desk at the campus library for two years," I said encouragingly. "It was part of my work-study program."

Maureen smiled kindly, but I could tell it hadn't added much weight to my argument.

"And I was the receptionist at a law firm for the last two summers," I added. "And—"

"Okay," Maureen held her hands up with a laugh. "I think you've convinced me. I want to see about moving you up from Brand Development immediately though. I go out on maternity leave in four weeks, and we'll need every day."

My heart leapt. Not only was she agreeing, but I was going to get away from Brand Development early? This was better than I'd hoped.

"Do you mind leaving Brand Development early?" she asked, knowing full well I didn't.

I shook my head so vehemently that she put a hand on her stomach and laughed. "I didn't think you would. Are there any loose ends you need to tie up? Projects to finish?"

I thought of the endless alphabetizing they'd been having me doing and the hours I'd just spent sitting behind various team members while they worked without bothering to explain what they were doing. "No projects."

Maureen looked unsurprised. "Not a very welcoming group, are they?"

I shook my head and shrugged. "No big deal. I was temporary."

"Well, I'll be glad to have you." Maureen glanced around. "I'll get another desk brought up. I need to talk to Con, and HR, but I'm hoping to have you in here by tomorrow."

"I could just stay," I said. "I'll pull up a chair and shadow you. I won't be in the way."

Maureen patted my arm. "I know you want out of Brand, but we have to go through Con and HR first."

My heart squeezed. This was the most delicate part of my plan, but I was counting on Maureen's influence to make it work. "What if he says no?"

He would absolutely say no. Hell no. I was taking a risk by trying to outmaneuver him. He might even follow through on his threat to try to drive me back to Ohio. But Maureen got a stubborn look on her face at the question. "He won't," she said determinedly. "This is the first plan that makes sense. If you're here and we get a good temp EA, I'll actually be able to relax on maternity leave. Or as much as newborns let you relax. I wouldn't know. They can't be more work than CEOs anyway"

I went back down to Brand Development, cautious optimism surging through me. If Maureen had her way, this would be the last time I walked through the chilly Brand offices.

And if Maureen had her way, I'd have mine, too, soon enough.

15

CON

"No fucking way," I told Maureen pleasantly. I wasn't going to yell at my pregnant EA. Not when she had kept my professional and personal obligations neatly organized for the last ten years, found a solution to every problem, and not once threatened to quit when shit got weird. And shit got weird a lot in this job.

She was like a sister to me, and I'd do anything for her.

But not this.

Maureen put her hands on her hips. "Con, this is the only fucking thing I've ever asked you for."

"That's not true," I said. "You ask me for things all the time."

She paused, considering it.

I leaned back in my chair and started ticking them off on my fingers. "You borrowed the apartment in Paris last year; I got you tickets to the *Charged Up* premiere last month, you took—"

"Okay fine, yes." Maureen smacked at my hand. One of the only people in the office who could have gotten away with it. "But I deserve all those things."

I laughed despite my annoyance. "Undoubtedly. But

you're not getting this. If you think you need two temps to replace you, we'll get two temps. You don't need Lily."

"Lily knows the agency better than a temp though. And I trust Lily. You could end up with two duds."

"Lily's been here a month. She doesn't know the agency any better than a temp."

"She knows you, though, and she's not intimidated." Maureen put her hands back on her hips and rocked her weight back, wincing slightly.

"Sit down, Mo." My jaw tightened, both with concern and at what she said. It would be better if Lily *was* intimidated, because I was starting to figure out where Maureen's insistence was coming from. Somehow, some way, Lily had put her up to this. "I won't intimidate the temp either," I said tightly.

Maureen sighed and tilted her head, assessing the look on my face. "Not on purpose. But you're intimidating, Con. I was scared to death of you the first few years I worked here."

"You were not," I said, affronted.

"Yes, I was. And it wasn't until I realized that you're not a complete asshole that I was able to really do my job well."

I paused, digesting this.

"Come on, Con." Maureen finally lowered herself into one of the chairs around my conference table, a hand carefully—and strategically—placed on her stomach that had risen like bread dough over the last few months. "I'll feel so much better if I have Lily and a temp covering you."

"Christ," I muttered. "Why don't you just come out and tell me I'll ruin your baby's first months of life if you don't get your way?"

Maureen smiled, knowing she had me. "I was saving it for the grand finale, but if I need to say it now..."

"No." I shook my head, frustration gnawing in my gut. I

was pissed, but not at Maureen. She was genuinely doing what she thought was best for me. It was Lily who deserved my wrath. And she'd get it.

But first, she was going to get her way.

Maureen went back to her desk to work things out with HR regarding Lily's new position. I stewed at my desk, coming up with a plan. I couldn't do anything until Maureen was out on maternity leave, but once she was, I'd deal with Lily. She might have been able to manipulate Maureen into forcing my hand, but once Maureen was out of the way, she'd have no one to hide behind.

* * *

I saw the desk being carried in and placed beside Maureen's. I saw IT set up the computer and printer. But I still wasn't prepared when I walked in on Tuesday morning and saw Lily sitting behind it all. I stopped dead, her physical presence hitting me like a blow. She was wearing a dress, but not one of the gauzy college-girl ones she'd tried to dress up with a blazer. This one was black and fitted, nipped in at the waist with a belt, and then swirling to a stop just above her knees. Perfectly appropriate for the office, and yet somehow seductive. She looked older than her twenty-three years in it, and I wondered if that was her goal.

"Good morning!" She leapt up when she saw me standing there. If she noticed my knuckles turning white around the handle of my briefcase, she didn't let on. "Can I get you some coffee?"

I breathed in slowly, released it. "Executive assistants don't get coffee."

"No?" Lily tilted her head so that the long golden sheets of hair slid off her shoulder.

"No," I said levelly. "I get my own. I think you'll find I'm fairly self-sufficient." And I was going to get more self-sufficient. I wasn't going to ask Lily to do a damn thing that brought her even a step closer.

She stepped closer anyway and blinked her wide, beautiful eyes. "Then what *do* I do?"

Was I imagining the coy note in her voice? I honestly couldn't fucking tell anymore. It didn't matter whether it was real or imagined though, lust was still slamming into me as I considered all the things she could do. With effort, I shoved the thoughts away and managed to say, "Keep my calendar straight and transfer my calls, and consider your job done."

I walked stiffly into my office, wishing for the first time that my door had a lock and that that two-thirds of the interior walls weren't fucking transparent. If I could have gotten some privacy, I'd have jerked off to the memory of her lips forming the question *what do I do?* And put her out of my mind.

Instead, I had to talk one client off a ledge over a perceived slight on set with my dick straining painfully against my pants. I stared at the back of Lily's blonde head and lost my train of thought more than once. Now I was the one pissing off my client.

"You're not even listening!" she yelled and hung up.

I couldn't argue that. She was an important client, but somehow, I couldn't remember a word she said. I didn't know whether to call up the director and tell him to give her a bigger trailer or the other actor's agent and rip him a new one. I slammed the phone down, frustration and something darker thrumming through me. I narrowed my eyes as Lily laughed at something Maureen had said. I couldn't hear her through the glass, but I imagined the throaty sound of it.

Thought of her profile picture again, those long, bare legs, the curve of her ass.

Three and a half more weeks, I told myself. Then Maureen would be out on maternity leave and Lily would be out on that perfect ass. After what she'd pulled, I'd take away everything. The job. The condo. I'd have to find a way to deal with Halley, but that seemed easy compared to the excruciating torture of being in close proximity with the one person I wanted that I couldn't have.

Why hadn't she just stayed the fuck away?

16

LILY

I'd spent my entire life playing by the rules, but something about Con brought out a recklessness in me that I hadn't known existed. Being around him was like a drug. Knowing that he was sitting behind that massive desk right behind me, playing kingmaker of Hollywood, kept me on the edge of my seat. Often, I imagined I could feel his eyes on me, but whenever I found a reason to turn to the side and sneak a glance back, he was looking somewhere else.

Aside from the first morning, I didn't get a moment alone with him. If he needed something, he called for Maureen. He always left for lunch. I didn't know if that was what he always did, or if it was a new habit he'd cultivated to avoid being left alone with me when Maureen went down to the cafeteria. I went with her more often than not. It gave us a chance to talk about the job, although I always tried to direct it to Con specifically.

"Does the job ever involve his personal life?" I asked, picking at my grilled chicken salad one day.

Maureen laughed. "You of all people should know the answer to that."

I looked up quickly, thinking at first she knew why I was so interested in his personal life. But there wasn't even a hint of a knowing glint in her eyes, and her smile was as open as ever.

"Haven't you and Halley called me often enough to get you out of jams?" she reminded me, poking my arm for emphasis. "Finding a dentist who spoke English in Prague definitely wasn't agency business."

I relaxed. Of course she was thinking about Halley. "Luckily I think Halley is staying put for a while," I said, and then revisited my original question, hoping for more information. "So his personal life *is* part of the job?"

I sounded too interested to my own ears, but Maureen didn't look suspicious as she considered the question. "It is sometimes," she said finally. "But the truth is, Con doesn't have much of a personal life. Sometimes you'll have to field calls from Kim, and once in a while he asks me to make a reservation. That's about it."

"I won't have to juggle multiple secret girlfriends?" I joked. "That's a relief."

I'd gone too far. Maureen tilted her head, hearing the inappropriate curiosity beneath the joke. "No," she said slowly. "You won't."

We fell silent. The low rumble of chatter and clanking silverware from the tables around us almost filled it, but not quite.

"How is Halley doing?" Maureen asked after a few long moments.

I swallowed. "She's good."

"She knows that..." Maureen trailed off and rubbed her belly absentmindedly while she figured out how to ask the question that was on her mind. I held my breath, afraid of what it might be. *She knows that you're obsessed with her father?*

"She knows that Con wouldn't hide anyone from her, doesn't she?" Maureen finished finally. "When he's serious about someone, she'll know it."

Relief filled me. She thought I was prying into Con's personal life at Halley's behest and not because of my own desperate curiosity.

"I think it's hard for her, being so far away," I said, careful not to brush her suspicion aside, lest she replace it with a different one that was closer to the truth. "I told her I'd keep an eye on him."

I felt a little sick, hearing how sincere I sounded. Who would have thought I had it in me? I certainly hadn't. And I didn't like it.

But no matter how many times I told myself that I had to stop, tell Maureen I didn't think I could handle the job, maybe even leave LA altogether, I could never follow through. My gaze would clash with Con's in an unguarded moment, and my knees would go weak.

When Angie Roberts, the temp, joined the office a week before Maureen went out on maternity leave, I really thought my chances of ever being alone with Con were gone. But unexpectedly, an opportunity fell in my lap. It was Tuesday evening. Con was already gone—he always left right at six on Tuesdays for some reason—when the courier came in with an impressively thick envelope that Maureen had to sign for.

"What is it?" I asked, trying to read the address label.

"A contract." Maureen frowned. "He must not have known it was coming. He usually wants to sign right away and get it sent back before someone changes their mind." She drummed her fingers on her desk, considering it. "Normally I'd run it by his place, but..." she trailed off, and rubbed her stomach. She hated saying that she was too tired to do something, but I knew she was.

I held my breath. I didn't dare suggest it, not after the close call in the cafeteria the other day, but I *hoped—*

Maureen sighed heavily, her brow wrinkling. "Lily, I hate to ask, but would you mind doing it for me? You don't have to wait for him. I'll give you his code, and you can just leave it on his desk. If he wants it sent back tonight, he'll call a courier."

"Sure, that's no problem," I said casually, hoping she couldn't hear my heart slamming against my ribs. "I don't mind waiting, either."

"No, don't do that." Maureen shook her head absently. "He goes to happy hour with his friends on Tuesday, so there's no telling when he'll be home."

I left the building clutching the padded envelope. I was worried I'd run into Con on the way out and lose my chance to go to his apartment, but I didn't. For once I was glad that he was nowhere to be seen. I went back to my condo first. I felt too keyed up to go straight to his place. If he'd answered the door, my nerves would have strangled me.

I poured myself a glass of wine. I'd finally bought my own bottles so I didn't have to keep making notes of things I needed to repay Halley for. While I drank it, I considered changing clothes. It figured that the one day I'd worn one of my old dresses from college would be the day I was sent to Con's apartment. In the end though, I decided to stay in what I was wearing. I didn't want to be too obvious. I was willing to put myself in his way, but he'd have to make the next move.

The wine did the trick of taking the edge off my nerves, and I headed down the street to the address Maureen had given me with a spring in my step. As it turned out his building was only one block from mine.

I was intimidated by the ornate lobby I stepped into. Even more so when a haughty concierge flanked by a burly security guard called, "Excuse me? Can I help you?" in a tone that clearly implied I was in the wrong place.

"I'm Lily Anderson," I said, hoping Maureen had remembered to let them know I was coming. "I have a package for Conall Walker."

Don't tell me to leave it here, I begged silently.

Luckily, the concierge just nodded and directed me to the elevator bank. There was a private one that went exclusively to his floor, and the concierge called for it from his desk. The carriage that carried me up twenty-four floors was absurdly luxurious. Marble tiles, a cut crystal chandelier, and velvet wallpaper. I couldn't help but run my fingers over the bristly gold walls, wondering if it was Con's style.

When it opened on his private lobby, I decided it wasn't. Con's space was the opposite of opulent. It was luxurious, but in a stripped down, austere way. He didn't have much furniture, but what he did have looked as though it had come out of the pages of a catalog. One that only millionaires should bother to subscribe to. The space was smaller than I expected, but I realized it was because the terrace that wrapped around his apartment was huge. The floor-to-ceiling windows of the living room, dining room, and kitchen all had the ability to roll up like garage doors, eliminating the division between indoor and outdoor. There were potted plants everywhere that replaced the usual trappings of a home.

I rubbed the leaf of a Ficus between my fingers, intrigued. Con had a few plants in his office, but I hadn't taken him for a gardener. But these all looked as though they'd been tended by an expert hand. I made a mental note to ask Halley about it, and then immediately discarded it. Even with the veneer of respectability that being sent here on an errand gave me, I didn't want Halley to have any reason to suspect I was interested in her father. Not for any reason.

Anything that happened between us had to stay a secret.

I found his office right where Maureen said it would be —in the back of the apartment across from a closed door that I assumed was his bedroom. The back of the place continued the inside-out theme. The wall was a sliding glass door from which I could see a putting green on the backside of the terrace. A lemon tree grew beside his desk, a small greenish fruit growing at the end of a branch, weighing it down.

I set the envelope down and felt a curious sense of disappointment. This was it. I was done with what I'd been sent to do. I was going to leave now, and everything would remain exactly as it was. Suspended between attraction and action. I walked out of his office reluctantly, but instead of going back toward the front, I reached for the knob of his bedroom door. I knew I shouldn't, but I couldn't resist. This might be my only chance to see his space. The way my plan was going, my job would be over before I got him to kiss me again. Much less do the things I dreamed about.

My nerves were jumping all up and down my spine as I turned the knob and pushed the door open slowly, half expecting to see him glaring back at me from the other side, asking what the fuck I thought I was doing. The room was empty though. Wide and spare. The dark gray flooring continued throughout. A king-sized bed that looked like something you'd find in a luxury hotel stood against one wall. It had crisp white sheets folded over a dark gray comforter. There was a sliding glass door that led out to the wrap around patio against one wall. Two armchairs with a small table between them in one corner. There was some sort of fern on the small table, but other than that, the room was curiously bare. It really did look like a hotel room instead of someone's bedroom.

Maybe that was why I felt emboldened to walk in. To walk all the way to the sliding glass doors and peek out through the wooden blinds at the view. That was where I was standing when I heard the elevator doors slide open in the lobby.

Panic balled itself up and lodged in my throat. I froze for a few crucial moments, ridiculous ideas running through my head. I could hide under the bed. No, there was no dust ruffle. He'd see me. I could try to let myself out onto the patio, but there was no way he wouldn't hear me. And what was my plan after that, exactly? To hide out there until he left for work tomorrow morning? I turned around, threw one panicked look at the bathroom, then flew across the room.

I didn't need to hide. I had a reason to be here. I just couldn't be caught in his bedroom. But my delay had cost me. I was just stepping out of the room when Con appeared at the mouth of the short hallway.

My mouth went dry at the sight of him. He'd never looked taller, broader, more imposing. There was a darkly incredulous look spreading across his face as he registered what door I was trying to pull shut behind me.

"Lily," he said, his voice almost pleasant but for the iron undertone. "What the fuck do you think you're doing?"

17

CON

Maureen texted me when I was at happy hour.

Courier arrived with a package. Contract(?). Sent Lily to your place with it. It'll be on your desk.

"Something the matter?" Landon asked astutely, seeing the expression on my face change.

"Nothing." I shoved my phone back in my pocket and picked up my beer. I tried to listen to whatever Dominic was saying, but my mind was warped by the image of Lily in my space. I had to keep my muscles tensed to keep them from springing into action and carrying me home to intercept her. It would be very, very stupid to try.

I downed my beer.

Or maybe I needed to go home and make sure she understood in no uncertain terms that she was never to come back. I didn't care if God himself ordered her to drop something off at my place, she had better leave it with the fucking concierge.

And then I remembered pulling up her Instagram page on my home computer a few nights ago. *Fuck.* Had I ever closed it out? Was there any chance at all that she would look at my computer? My home one wasn't password protected. An oversight I would correct immediately.

"I have to go," I said suddenly, breaking into Dominic's story. The odds of Lily waking up my computer and her Instagram profile still being up on the screen were about as slim as the anorexic model selling lipstick on the billboard across the street, but I still couldn't take the risk.

Dominic nodded goodbye and launched right back into his story. Not much could stop Dominic when he was on a roll. The others said quick goodbyes and went back to listening—all except Landon, who gave me an inscrutable look.

"What?" I asked, signaling the bartender for my check.

"You're in a hurry all of a sudden."

"What's wrong with that?"

He shrugged, like he was waiting for me to answer that question. He knew it had something to do with Lily. Landon seemed to always know shit like that. It was why he was such a good security expert. He could get inside people's heads.

I didn't want him in my head though, not now. There were things in there I couldn't even let my best friends see.

"Some of us have to hustle for a living," I deflected. "A big contract just came in, and I have to get it squared away before the actress thinks of anything else to ask for."

"So it's a demanding woman?" Landon asked, knowing full well I was bullshitting him. I had over explained myself, a mistake he always caught onto.

"Exactly." I signed the credit card slip and left before Landon could continue his line of questioning.

I got back to my place in record time. When I got there, my eyes swept the lobby warily for any sign of Lily. Had I missed her? Was she on her way out? How would I deliver the message that I had for her in public? What was the socially acceptable way to say *stay the fuck out before I do something we'll both regret?*

I didn't have to worry about it. She wasn't in the lobby, nor was she in the elevator when it arrived. That meant she could either teleport, or she was still in my penthouse. The thought of her in my space stirred emotions I didn't want to bother identifying. Not until I was back in the shower anyway.

When I stepped out of the elevator on the top floor, I knew she was in there. I could sense her. I moved through the penthouse silently. No sign of her in the living room or the kitchen. Then I saw her. I almost wasn't surprised when I found her in the last place she should be, stepping out of my bedroom, her movements quick and furtive. Not quick enough though.

When she saw me, she dropped the knob like it was evidence.

"I–I was just looking for the bathroom," she stammered.

She was a beautiful liar and sneak. Guilt made her cheeks flush and her eyes wide. Her chest was rising and falling distractingly.

I stepped forward, deliberately crowding her back. Then I opened the door myself and looked in. Not a thing was out of place, but she'd disturbed it all the same. She'd disturbed *me.*

"I came back here to tell you to stay the fuck out of my space," I said, almost to myself.

"I was curious," Lily whispered, abandoning the pretense.

My hand tightened on the knob. "You should have stayed away, Lily. You really should have."

"I couldn't."

Giving up the pretense, she touched my arm, carefully, lightly. Weeks of pent-up frustration were coursing through my veins. I couldn't hold myself back anymore. I wanted her more than I'd ever wanted any other woman in my life, and she was giving me permission. Fuck all the rest.

I shoved the door open, hard. Lily jumped in surprise and took another step back.

"Oh no you don't." I yanked her to me, wrapping one arm around her waist so that the length of her body was imprinted against mine. I tangled my free hand in her hair and pulled her head back so that I could look down into her face. I needed to make sure she understood the rules of what she was signing up for.

"I want to fuck you," I said, forcing all tenderness out of my voice. "But that's all this can be. I can't be your boyfriend."

"Who said I want you to be?" Lily asked rebelliously. "I've had a lot of boyfriends, Con. You're not exactly someone I could bring home."

My grip tightened instinctually at the part about *a lot of boyfriends.* "I'm going to make you forget about all of them," I swore, and crushed her mouth with mine.

Anger and lust made for a toxic and intoxicating combination. I backed her up into my bedroom, but instead of walking her back to my bed, I pushed her up against a wall and continued my assault on her mouth. I wanted her to know that this wasn't going to be romantic. There wouldn't be any candlelight and roses.

To my surprise, she didn't try to soften the kiss. To my relief and disappointment, she didn't push me away either and call me an asshole. Instead, she seemed to revel in the brutality, wrapping her arms around my neck and offering her willing young body up for more. She was wearing one of her older dresses, one of the drifty, diaphanous ones that sunlight cut right through. I pulled it up from the hem, pushing it up over her waist and pinning the fabric there between our bodies. She gasped when I slid my hand into her panties. She was already hot and wet, practically dripping on my fingers. Part of me wanted to push her down to the floor right now and slide myself in. She was ready.

But I wouldn't be able to control myself. I'd jackhammer into her, and it would be over in five minutes. That didn't work for me. If I was going to hell, I wanted to take my time getting there.

"Con," Lily moaned when I slid a finger into her slippery, velvety box. I looked down at her while I pumped another finger in. Her eyes were heavy lidded with lust, unfocused. She still had her arms wrapped around my neck, but her fingers were loosely knit. I had a feeling that it was the pressure of my body against hers keeping her up.

"Tell me about all those ex-boyfriends now," I taunted quietly. "Did any of them make you feel like this?"

She shook her head, the movement languid. She bit down on her lower lip hard, and her head fell back as I found the sensitive nub of her clit and tweaked it.

"Tell me what you want, Lily." I leaned in to nip her earlobe.

"I want you," she whispered.

"You want me to what?" I was going to make her say it. She'd pushed us to this point. She had to go the rest of the way.

"I want you–" her eyes opened slowly. I was still fingering her, and I could see the unbearable tension of mounting lust in her blue gaze. "--I want you inside me."

"I am inside you." I pushed a third finger in to prove the point. God, she was tight. She was going to squeeze my cock like a vice. I couldn't wait.

Her body trembled, eyes drifting closed again. "You know what I mean."

"No." I stilled, withdrew. "No acting like a shy college

girl, Lily. Tell me exactly what you want or go the hell home."

Her eyes flew open. I saw the same desperation I felt in the depths. I'd make her leave if I had to, but I had a feeling I wouldn't.

"I want your–" her cheeks flushed deeper, "--cock in my mouth."

I'd already been ready, but now all the blood flowed downward, leaving me lightheaded and painfully hard. It was all I could do to take a step back as she slid down my body to her knees and looked up at me, grasping my manhood just the way I'd imagined the other night.

"Lily," I groaned, bracing myself against the wall to keep from slamming my hips forward as she gently slid her lips over the tip.

She bobbed up and down, almost gingerly. "I've never done this before," she whispered.

A better man would have ended it right then. I wasn't that man. I put a hand gently on the back of her head and guided her up and down. I'd been sucked off by near pros, but nothing had ever felt as good as Lily's tongue swirling gently around my shaft, her hands on either side of my hips. I closed my eyes and reveled in it. Then, when I couldn't stand it anymore, I pulled back.

She looked up at me uncertainly.

I pulled her to her feet and undid the zipper that ran down her back. Her dress fell off like a flower shedding its petals, leaving her in two scraps of lace that I knew wouldn't last another minute.

"Let's go," I murmured, and led her to the bed.

18

LILY

I followed Con as if in a daze. His fingers were wrapped tightly around mine, and something seemed to have shifted in him. When he pulled me to him beside the bed, his caress was gentler. He'd stopped raging against whatever force was pulling us inexorably together, stopped fighting my existence in his life, his penthouse, his bedroom. He ran his hands up my bare arms, making me shiver.

There was something I should tell him, but I couldn't bring myself to do it. He might stop if I did. If he knew he was going to be my first. He might make it into something bigger than it was and force himself to do the *right thing*. This was the right thing though. I knew it in my bones, the way I'd known that every boy before him who I'd come close with hadn't been right. Hadn't been enough.

So instead of speaking, I touched him. I took advantage of his new calm and ran my hands over the thick ridges of muscles that made up his torso. Smoothed them over his pectorals and over his strong, corded shoulders. He undid the clasp of my bra and slid the thin straps over my shoulders until it fell between us. Then he pushed down the matching panties, and I was standing in front of him naked.

That was a first in itself.

The sun slanted in. Funny how I'd always assumed my first time would be at night, in the dark. This was so much better. I could see every inch of him. The minute changes in the rise and fall of his chest as he drank me in. The way his eyes narrowed and darkened. The coarse dark hair that made a line down his abdomen. The quiver in his hands as he reached for me.

When he kissed me again, it was gentler too. Slower, even as he lifted me and set me on the bed. My heart beat wildly. It was happening. It was really happening. After all these weeks of waiting and wishing and wanting, I was going to have Con.

I laid back, pulling him with me. He was propping himself up on one arm, his other hand holding my wrist, pinning it to the bed. There was a cloud of pillows behind me, his warm, heavy weight on top of me. His knee was between my legs, his hard on like a rock against my leg, but neither of us wanted to rush it. We explored each other's bodies with our hands, our mouths. I tasted his throat, nibbled on his shoulders, scraped my teeth lightly over his clavicle. His tongue was doing an erotic dance in my ear that I felt radiating through my entire body. Along with the sensations, emotions were rushing through me. Relief, joy, disbelief. It was finally happening. Short of the end of the world, nothing would stop me from making Con Walker my first.

When I flicked my tongue into his ear, his hand tightened around my wrist. "I need to get inside you," he whispered, his voice sounding heavy and drugged.

I tensed as I felt him adjust, lining up his manhood and nudging it gently against my opening. I held my breath and gripped onto him with the hand he wasn't pinning to the bed. His skin was damp with perspiration. He slid in, easily at first.

"You're so tight," he said thickly. "Fuck, you feel so good. I just want to—"

"You can," I whispered into his shoulder, squeezing my eyes shut and bracing myself. He pushed the full length of his shaft into me, taking my virginity in one swift thrust. A sharp pain had me crying out, but then a wave of pleasure swept it away. He hesitated, but then I wrapped my legs around his, refusing to let him pull away.

"Don't stop," I begged. "Not now."

With a muttered oath, Con's control broke and he began moving his hips, harder and faster. The waves of pleasure built higher, wiping out even the memory of the initial pain. I gripped onto him tighter, moaning his name over and over, stretching around his cock, taking it deeper and deeper.

I climaxed hard, gasping his name, black tinging the edges of my vision. Then I saw his eyes go black, the irises eclipsed by the pupils as he came. His hips pumped once, twice more, as he emptied himself into me.

Then he collapsed onto me and we lay entwined, hearts pounding together. He would have questions later, I was sure. But for now, neither of us had any words left. We'd exhausted each other, and as the sun slipped below the horizon, we fell asleep in each other's arms.

* * *

I woke up the next morning to the sound of the shower. For a minute, I was disoriented. Who was in my condo? Had Halley come back? And then the memory of my night with Con flared in my head, chasing out the fog of sleep. I rolled over in his large bed and touched a hand to the indentation beside me. Still warm. I dropped my forehead to the sleek, silky sheets and inhaled. His cologne was faint but spicy in my nostrils, and it created a visceral memory of his hands on my body. Sensation raced through me, but not enough to drive out the concern niggling deep in my heart.

What would Halley think?

The shower went off, the hard spray reducing to loud, pattering droplets. I heard the glass door slide open. I pulled on my dress and considered slipping out as quickly as possible, but before I could take stock of where the rest of my clothes had ended up, the bathroom door was opening. Con stood in the doorway, backlit by the bright overhead, a towel banded around his waist.

Our eyes met. His gaze was implacable and impossible to read.

"Why didn't you tell me?" he asked.

Heat leapt to my cheeks. I hoped he couldn't see my flush in the watery morning light streaming in behind me. "I didn't want it to matter," I said honestly.

A crack of emotion, quickly concealed. He tightened the towel. "I had a right to know."

"Why? So you could use it as another excuse to put off what we both knew was inevitable?" I rose up to my knees in the sumptuous bed and put my hands on my hips. "Did you want me to go out and lose my virginity to just anyone before you were willing to—"

"Don't even think about finishing that sentence, Lily" he said harshly. I could see the cords of muscle in his crossed arms tense.

"What's this really about?" I pushed him. "Do you want me to have more experience? Should I—"

Con crossed the room in a few steps and grabbed me by the arms. His strength immobilized me even though the pressure of his fingers on my skin was carefully controlled.

130

My face was beneath his, and his dark eyes bored down into mine. "Don't ever talk to me about going out and getting more experience with other men again," he said in a deadly quiet voice I'd never heard him use.

Though his tone and overwhelming physical presence should have intimidated me, I swayed closer. His chest was still damp. The droplets seeped quickly through the thin material of my dress. My nipples peaked and hardened as his hands slid up my arms, over my shoulders, up into my hair until he was holding my face between them. His words still hung in the air, underlined by the harsh rasp of his breath. I wanted to close my eyes and give into the sensations flooding through my body, but his dark gaze pinned mine, making it impossible to look away.

"I won't," I whispered so quietly that if there had been more than a few inches between my lips and his ears, he wouldn't have heard me. It didn't even occur to me to play games like I'd seen other girls do and ask him why not. We both knew. I was his. He might not be mine—not yet anyway—but I was his. I'd given him more than my virginity, whether he wanted it or not.

From the look on his face, I could tell he wasn't sure which it was. His body wanted me; I could feel that clearly enough. The struggle was in his mind, between the primitive, carnal part of his brain and the part that remembered what consequences were.

Later, I slipped out of Con's building with my heart pulsing in my throat. I could practically taste the adrenaline all the way up the block. My heartbeat was just returning to normal when my smart watch vibrated on my wrist, and I looked down to see Halley's name.

She knows.

Sick guilt washed through me, nearly driving out the afterglow of my stolen morning hours with Con. But not quite. I took a deep, steadying breath. There was no way that Halley knew. Sure, I could chase my paranoia down a rabbit hole of *but maybe someone she knew saw me in the lobby yesterday and again just now, and they put two and two together, and now she's just gotten off the phone with them, and she's calling me to tell me I'm the worst friend ever.*

Pure speculation. Would never hold up. I clamped down on it hard before I could spin this into an even more dramatic tale. My watch was still vibrating, and I was still staring at her name, trying to make a decision. Instantly, my mind put me on the witness stand. What would an innocent person do?

The answer was easy. They'd answer the phone, same as always. Breezy voice. *You're up early.* The cross examination would only have something to bite down on if the behavior deviated from normal. *Why didn't you answer your best friend's phone call or return it? Weren't you living in her condo?*

Before my paranoia could well up again, I fished my phone out of my purse and answered it on the third ring.

"You're up early," I said, my voice more croaky than breezy.

"You sound sick," Halley said. "Is my dad working you too hard?"

I tried not to choke, remembering how hard we'd worked each other last night. To the breaking point and beyond. My inner thighs ached even as I moistened, remembering. "No. I'm just—," I cleared my throat. "I'm just tired."

"Late night?" Halley's voice carried the typical insinuation those two words produced. God, if she only knew, I thought in dismay.

I tried to cover it with a laugh. "No—just." I searched

frantically for a plausible reason, a legitimate excuse, and found nothing. "I'm just tired," I finished lamely.

"Huh, well, I don't believe you, but that's okay. You'll tell me in a month when I come visit you!"

Birds rose up in a startled flock in the small green space that passed for a park in front of my building. A small dog yipped delightedly, leaping up and snapping at their tail feathers even though they were already twenty feet in the air. I stared at the scene, dazed. Halley was coming to visit in a month? Why not anytime in the last several weeks when I was desperate for her? Why now, when I finally had—

My mind flat out would not let my thoughts go to *her father*.

"Lily, did you hear me?" Halley prompted. "I'm coming to visit in October for the long weekend."

"Columbus Day?"

"Indigenous People's Day, you monster."

I laughed again. This time it was real and appropriate, but it sounded weak even to my own ears. "That's awesome. I can't wait to see you."

"We'll have to play tour guide for each other," she said enthusiastically. "I bet you've found all kinds of new, fun places to show me. Maybe with that mysterious guy who I *know* is the reason you're acting so flaky."

"Uh, yeah." I was still watching the birds gliding to a different curated green space, their black wings spread wide, flashing across the landscape of high rises and the vertical slices of bright blue sky separating them. Then I processed what she'd said and laughed again, this time with a little more strength. "Actually, you're going to be disappointed. LA Lily is the same as college Lily. I spend most of my time working, and I don't know any spots hotter than the local coffee shop."

"Then I'll take you to my spots," Halley said confidently. "You have to have some fun while you're in LA, Lily. I know it's all about the end game for you, but life is a journey too, you know."

Some fun. Again, I was in Con's bed. Again, I hated myself for it. I went on the offensive. "Speaking of life and end games, why doesn't your dad know you want to act?"

I realized too late that I was giving her a reason to ask suspiciously, *why are you and my dad so close all of a sudden?* But Halley just blew her breath out, not suspicious at all. "You don't know my dad. Well," she considered, "maybe you do now. But he'd hate it if he knew I was planning to act. He thinks there are too many narcissists and predators in the industry."

I thought about the news stories lately. "He's not wrong," I said. "But surely his reputation would protect you."

Halley answered, but I wasn't listening. I was thinking about what Con said before. About how he was *just like them.* Was he talking about the Weinsteins of the industry? Did he think he was like them because he had slept with me? He couldn't though—it was absurd. He hadn't lured me into a hotel room under the guise of a business meeting. I'd practically broken into his apartment and waylaid him. If anyone was Weinstein, it was me.

"Anyway," Halley continued, "I'd appreciate it if you didn't say anything. I mean, I know he suspects because he insisted I graduate college before I make any life decisions, and normally like, what you major in *is* a life decision, right? So he knows. He just doesn't want to. And that's fine. He can live in ignorance, and I—"

She was off again, in typical Halley fashion. Her steady, comforting monologues had been my bedtime stories when we shared a room in the sorority house. Halley had a knack for knowing when to talk and when to listen, and now, somehow, she knew I didn't want to talk. Probably because she was my best friend.

When we got off the phone, I made a half-hearted resolution to myself. I would *never* let her find out about her father and me. I'd take that secret to the grave. I pictured a long line of years in front of us, the three of us and this secret. I saw myself running into him at her wedding. Nodding along when she mentioned him, pretending like my interest was only polite and not avid. I even let my brain venture into the painful territory of hearing that he had finally met someone Halley didn't hate. That they were engaged.

My heart cracked at the idea, and I pulled back from it sharply.

No, there was no reason to borrow trouble like this. All I had to do was keep my promise to myself that Halley would never find out about us. Anything that came after—well, I'd take it as it came.

19

CON

I made the decision as soon as Lily left. I had to get her out of my life before this happened again. I should have never let things go so far between us. And I never would have if I'd known it was her first time. At least, that was what I told myself. I couldn't explain why I'd done it a second time, and then a third, other than to say that she went to my head. I didn't think straight around her, and now I really fucking needed to untangle this mess. I'd never been with a virgin–Kim had been my first though I hadn't been hers–but I was pretty sure it meant something when one chose you. Meant something more than I was prepared to give.

The first step to getting Lily out of my life was to get her out of my office. I made a call to the top celebrity divorce lawyer in town to see if I could arrange an internship for Lily in her office. She'd represented several of my clients, and we'd been friends for years. We'd crossed the line between friends and lovers a few times, but neither of us had ever been interested in more.

"Well, if it isn't Con Walker," she said when she answered the phone. "Who is it this time?" There was relish in her voice. Laura loved a good divorce. The nastier the better.

"It's not about a divorce," I said.

"Oh?" her voice downshifted into a purr. "If this isn't about business, is it about pleasure?"

"Not exactly." I gave Laura the situation straight. I'd considered playing it as just trying to call in a favor for my daughter, then rejected the deception for two reasons. One, it wasn't necessary. Laura and I had shared a few nights. Nothing to get possessive over. Two, Laura was a seasoned professional at detecting bullshit. Nothing would piss her off more than to discern that I was lying to protect her feelings when she didn't have any worth protecting. At least not where I was concerned.

"Oh Con," she laughed, and the sound was rich and throaty. "Oh, you've really done it now. I thought you were smarter than that."

"I thought so too," I said grimly. "We were both wrong."

"She's going to law school?"

"Yeah, she got in this year. She deferred for financial reasons. That's why Halley asked me to give her a job and a place to stay." I drummed my fingers on my desk, my gaze returning to the front door. Where the hell was Lily? And why was I so anxious to see her when the whole point of this phone call was to never see her again?

"So nice of you to give her all that and *more*," Laura said.

My unamused silence didn't stop her from laughing again.

"Okay, okay. I'll stop," she said. "Listen, I don't need an intern, but I do need a receptionist. Think you can sell her on that?"

"I think she'll be there tomorrow. Thanks, Laura." I hung up the phone just as Lily came in. She'd changed into a black pants suit that somehow managed to accentuate her curves, making her look less and less like the college girl she'd been when she got here. Now she looked like a full-blooded woman. Or maybe it was my perception that had changed since I'd made her one, taking the last vestiges of girlhood. Whatever it was, she looked too damn good to stay.

I buzzed her. "Lily, can you come to my office for a minute?"

She'd just hung her purse on the hook and was saying good morning to Angie. Now she looked up and met my eyes through the glass. It was a cliche to call it a deer in the headlights expression, but that was exactly what it was. Eyes wider than Bambi's, lips parted in surprise. She made her way around to the door, let herself in, and turned around to face me, still holding the handle with one hand.

"I'm not going to bite," I said brusquely.

Her cheeks flushed, and I remembered that I'd bitten last night. Nipped the soft flesh, tasted. I looked away, jaw clenching as I tried to get a grip on myself. "This isn't going to work," I said tightly, directing my words to the Ficus beside my desk. "I can't have you here. Not after..." I looked back to see her face was now very pale.

"What do you mean?" Lily asked, her voice trembling. "Are you seriously firing me after–?"

I cut her off before she could get to what came *after*. "No, I'm giving you a better opportunity. My friend is a top divorce lawyer in this town. She needs a receptionist. It'll be a good way to learn the business. Better than you could get here."

Lily's eyes had lost their focus. I couldn't tell if she was looking at me or through me, and I had no idea what was running through her head as she listened to me list all the reasons this would be better.

"It's not about any of that though, is it?" she said quietly when I was done. "It's about us."

"It's about there not being an us," I corrected. "Last night was a mistake."

Lily lifted her chin, her eyes snapping to life again the way they did when I pissed her off. "And this morning?"

I exhaled in frustration. "Another fucking mistake, Lily. That's why I can't have you around. I'm going to keep making mistakes with you, and I don't want to be that asshole."

"And you think firing me—"

"Reassigning you," I corrected.

"--makes you, what, a standup guy?" Her blue eyes were blazing now, but she kept her voice quietly controlled.

"No, I don't think it makes me a standup guy," I said, struggling to keep my own voice from rising. My hands balled into fists with the effort of keeping them to myself. Even as I was trying to send her away, I wanted to drag her closer. Why had I succumbed to this open concept office bullshit? If I had a wall instead of a window between my office and the reception area, I could touch her.

And the fact that I was still thinking about touching her was the reason she had to go.

"I'm not a standup guy," I said, my voice low and rough. "We both know that. That's another reason why you'll be better off with Laura."

"Fine," Lily said, clipping her syllables. "But if you think that's going to solve the problem, you're wrong."

I didn't say anything as she turned on her heel and walked out. Of course it would solve the problem. It would take a few days, but eventually, the old principle of out of sight, out of mind would take effect. I turned back to my computer, trying to ignore the shape of her in my peripheral vision.

Just a few more days, I told myself.

* * *

Lily disappeared at lunch. I told myself I was glad. But when I saw her sitting in the cafeteria with a guy from the media rights advisory team, my fingers curled into fists again. I knew Devon just well enough to know I didn't like him. I made a mental note to fire him the next time he so much as forgot to return a phone call.

Lily was laughing at something he was saying, and the slant of sunlight she sat in gilded her golden skin and hair. She looked luminous, and Devon couldn't keep his eyes off her. I'd planned to grab a quick bite here, but now I decided to go out.

I was back at my desk with my sandwich when Lily came back from lunch. Angie, Maureen's temp, was still out, so the two of us were effectively alone. Lily had a small smile on her lips, and her cheeks were flushed the way they'd been after I kissed her the first time. Had she let that prick Devon kiss her? I imagined the two of them alone in the elevator, his hands on her, and my whole body turned to stone. Forget waiting for a missed phone call, I'd fire him now.

Our gazes caught, and I was glad there was glass between us. She jolted slightly when she saw me at my desk. She'd expected me to still be out the way I usually was. Then the smile dropped from her lips. She raised her eyebrows—half challenge, half question.

My finger itched to press the intercom button and call her in. I'd tell her that if she so much as passed Devon in the lobby, he'd never work in this town again. But if I took the leash off my temper long enough to do that, there was no telling what else I might do if I had Lily alone again.

A long moment stretched between us, and I had a feeling she knew exactly what I was debating. She was waiting to see which side would win out—the one that couldn't resist her or the one that had to.

I was waiting too.

But before either side could win the tug of war, the door behind her opened and Angie came in. Lily broke eye contact to look over at her and smile. I kept my eyes on the back of Lily's golden head and wondered how many times we'd find ourselves back in this exact situation.

And how I would continue to keep my hands off her.

20

LILY

Devon was a nice guy. He was a slightly older, more mature version of the boys I'd dated throughout high school and college. Earnest, kind, with a broad, open face that made you feel like you could trust anything he said. I used to be a sucker for that. He held doors open for me and carried my lunch tray. He told me he was from the Midwest. He thought one day he'd move back. This place wasn't really for him. He was thirty-one, which would have seemed like a vast age difference if I hadn't lost my virginity to a forty-year-old last night. Now it seemed too young. And he was *too* earnest. Every kind thing he did made me miss Con's brusque nature. The contrast between his abrasive public self and the tenderness beneath that so few people got to see. Still, I asked Devon if he wanted to get a drink after work.

I felt guilty. I'd found the nicest guy in LA, and I was using him. It was working though. I saw how Con stopped dead when he saw us sitting together in the cafeteria. Later, in his office, his gaze had scorched mine. He was jealous. And if he was jealous, that meant he cared.

At the end of the workday, Devon came up to get me.

142

When he came down the hall from the elevator bank and saw me, he smiled at me then back at Con, who was still at his desk. I didn't dare turn to see the look on Con's face as I stood up and grabbed my purse, but I saw Devon's smile falter.

My stomach swooped pleasantly. I wished it was because of the way Devon's golden brown eyes settled on mine appreciatively, but it was a direct result of the anger I sensed simmering in the man behind me. I didn't understand myself anymore. The nicest man in LA was holding out his arm for mine, and I wanted to go back to the asshole who had slept with me and then re-homed me like a puppy he'd adopted then decided he didn't have enough time for.

"Where do you want to go?" Devon asked as we waited for the elevator.

For a second, I was speechless, thinking he'd read my mind. Where did I want to go? Back to Con, but how did he know? But before I could make a fool of myself, Devon went on, "If you want to go somewhere that we can grab dinner at after, I know a good place."

Of course that was what he meant. Disappointment and relief churned in my stomach. "I'd love dinner," I lied.

* * *

We went to an all-American place that served burgers and malts and hot, crinkly, crispy French fries that tasted like being back in Ohio. It was a world away from the intimidating steakhouse that Con had taken me to for lunch. I liked it better. I would have loved it if it had been Con sitting across from me instead of Devon.

Devon walked me back to my building after dinner. I didn't invite him up, and he didn't seem to expect it. He didn't mention going out again either. I wasn't surprised. I'd tried to keep up my facade, but I hadn't been successful. It wasn't in me to play these games. Not with Devon, who didn't deserve them. Not even with Con, who absolutely deserved to be played. But not by me. I deserved a man who didn't need games.

It felt good to realize that as I rode the elevator up to the thirtieth floor. Empowering. But then I remembered that it didn't matter what I deserved—what I *wanted* was Con. My head was aching with the pressure of all my conflicting desires by the time I let myself into Halley's condo. It was just now getting dark outside, but all I wanted to do was go to bed.

I dropped my purse by the front door and didn't even bother to turn on the lights as I made my way down the narrow hall, past the kitchen. I was thinking about climbing into bed, sliding between the cool sheets, and pulling the blanket over my head when suddenly, the living room light snapped on.

I froze mid-stride. My first instinct was to scream, but my heart had slammed up into my throat at the *click* of the rotary switch. It was throbbing there, cutting off my breath, as warm, rosy light spilled through the room. There was a man sitting beside it. Incongruously tall, lean, and masculine against the fluffy white chair. He rose, his face a tightly controlled mask.

"Con," I breathed, my heart slipping back into place. It was still pounding like crazy, and a hundred different emotions circulated through my bloodstream. Lingering fear, relief, and excitement led the pack. "You scared me."

He looked indifferent, as though it didn't matter that he'd nearly given me a heart attack. "You're back early." He crossed the room, slowly closing up the space between us.

I took a small step back. It was funny how I was always seeing new sides to Con. I'd thought I'd seen him mad

144

before, but I realized those had all been more pallid versions of his anger. *This* was what he looked like when he was mad. It wasn't when his brows were slanted together, or his mouth was a flat line or even when he was blowing out his breath in aggravation. It was this eerily calm, impeccably controlled man I saw before me. *This* was his anger. I should have been afraid, but somehow, I was only compelled. I had a feeling that I was seeing something that very, very few people had ever gotten to see. This was how storm chasers must feel when a tornado touched down in front of them. More exhilarated than terrified, accepting the clear and present danger because the payoff was worth it.

"It was just dinner," I said, bumping against the edge of the island. "Nothing more."

Con's lips curved upward, but it couldn't have been called a smile by any stretch of the imagination. It was the opposite of a smile. A black hole into which all light was crushed. "Lucky for him." He took another step closer.

I shifted back, but there was nowhere left to go. When his arms locked onto the counter on either side of mine, caging me in, I didn't even try to escape. I lifted my chin instead. "Not that it's any business of yours."

"You're my business, Lily."

Though his face was just above mine, his voice somehow sounded disembodied. His broad shoulders blocked the light of the lamp. I could smell the faint musk of his cologne. He was so close I could see his heartbeat pulsing in the hollow of his throat. I tipped my head back and met his eyes. Dark, boring down into mine. I was heady from his nearness, still dizzy from the shock of him being here. My knees felt weak, but I *wasn't* going to give in this easily.

"Either I'm your business, or I'm a mistake," I said quietly. "I'm not going to be both."

The cords of muscle in his arms, visible beneath his rolled-up sleeves, tensed as he tightened his grip on the counter. "What else could this be?" he asked harshly. "You're—"

"I know all the reasons," I interrupted, deflecting the pain that threatened to skewer my heart all over again, the way it had this morning. "But it doesn't feel like a mistake to me." I wanted to be strong, but I knew my gaze had become imploring. I reached up and touched his face, wishing that terrible mask would crack. "Does it really feel like one to you?"

Con jerked away from the gentle pressure of my fingers on his jawline. Tears leapt into my eyes. "I guess so," I whispered and tried to push out of the cage of his arms. His arms were like iron bars though, and the more I struggled, the harder he pressed me back against the bar until I was trapped, pinned there like a butterfly. Even through the pain in my heart, my body registered how good his felt against mine. Reacted. His was reacting too. I felt his hard on against my hip, heard his breathing change. He locked his arms around me and held me hard against him, trying to subdue my attempt to struggle away.

"Maybe you're not my mistake," he said, his hands tangling in my hair at the base of my neck. He pulled my head back, his dark eyes devouring every inch of my face, my throat, lingering at the place where my breasts were pressed against his hard chest. "But I'm yours. I'm too old for you. Not good for you. I can't offer you a future."

"I don't care," I whispered.

My words seemed to release something in him. They ended his struggle. Before the last one was even out of my mouth, his was crushing down on mine. Relief swept through me. It was like I'd been holding my breath for hours, my lungs about to burst, and now sweet oxygen was filling my lungs. I couldn't get enough of him. I wanted to feel him everywhere, his skin against mine, his hair twined in my fingers. I needed him to fill me the way he had last night. He deepened the kiss, his tongue thrusting against mine, and I could taste his desperation. Knew he felt the same way.

I clawed at the buttons of his shirt until he pushed my ineffectual hands away and undid the buttons himself. Then he broke our kiss to reach down and grab the hem of my black dress, yanking it up to my waist, and then over my head. I'd spent a small fortune on the embroidered black bra with strategically sheer lace and the matching v-string that I was wearing, but he barely seemed to notice them. His eyes burned into mine as he stripped off the rest of his clothes and stood before me, hard and naked. A sculpted figure in the lamp light. My breath caught. Even though I'd seen him like this just this morning, his size still unnerved me. Heat rushed to pool between my legs, my body assuring me I could take his.

My heart beating fast, I reached behind me to unsnap my bra. Hesitated. Even though he'd seen *me* like this just this morning, my nerves still hummed to life.

"Take it off," he said quietly. His eyes darkened further at the sight of my bare breasts released from the embroidered cups. They rose to mine. "I don't think I can be gentle tonight," he said, half warning, half promising.

In answer, I rolled the absurdly small scrap of black fabric that was the panties down over my hips, kicked them aside.

Con pulled me to him, and I felt the tension in his hands as they skimmed over my naked back to my buttocks. He squeezed hard, still holding back. I pressed against him eagerly, wrapping my arms around his neck and rubbing against his hard cock, ready to be filled by it again. He shook his head though and led me around to the couch.

"Sit down."

I sat and reached for him, but he shook his head again and huffed out a strange laugh. "No, if I feel your lips on my cock, it's over. We're going to try something different."

To my surprise, he knelt down in front of me and parted my knees, fitting himself between them.

"You've never done this before, have you?" he asked, lowering his mouth to my inner thigh.

Wordlessly, I shook my head.

His eyes gleamed with satisfaction. "Good. I want to be your first everything."

Everything? But I only had a moment to wonder what else *everything* consisted of before he reached up with one hand to squeeze my breasts while his tongue flicked into me. Sensation hit me like a Mack truck. I moaned, knotting one fist in his hair, grabbing the edge of the couch with the other.

"Does it feel good, baby?" Con asked, his voice almost taunting. He had to see that my eyes were rolled back in my head. I could barely speak. He didn't give me a chance anyway. He was doing figure eights with his tongue and each swipe against my clit pushed me closer to orgasm.

"Yes," I managed to moan. "But I want you inside me."

"Didn't I teach you anything last night?" He pushed two fingers in, pumping relentlessly. "You can have multiple orgasms. I'm the one who has to pace himself."

He made me come twice just from his mouth and fingers. Then he stood up, rock hard, his whole body quivering with the tension of holding himself back to focus on my pleasure. Though seconds before, I'd felt boneless and sated, I felt my desire surge back.

"My turn," I whispered, sliding down onto my knees in front of him.

Con's hands knotted around my shoulders, and he pulled me up. "No," he rasped. "I need to fuck you now."

He gave me a hard, bruising kiss, then turned me around and pushed me over to the side of the couch. "Bend over."

I bent over and grabbed the arm of the couch for support, my nerves coming back.

Con pushed into me, from behind his cock stretching me almost to the point of pain. He wrapped his large hands around my waist, and I sensed he was holding himself back. Letting me adjust. I nudged back against him, letting him know I was ready. That I wanted more.

His hands tightened, and then he began to rock his hips back and forth. I squeezed my eyes shut; the pleasure almost unbearable. I was making keening noises I'd never heard myself make before. In between, begging him for more.

"You like it like this?" he asked, plowing into me harder.

I nodded desperately, though my head was already bouncing around from the force of his thrusts. "Yes, *yes*," I said, almost pleading. I'd never imagined sex could be like this. Animalistic in its passion but still somehow safe. Con could have asked me to do anything, and I would have done it eagerly.

"I can't believe I'm the only man who has gotten to see you like this," he said almost to himself.

"You're the. Only one. I've ever wanted like this," I managed to say. Mounting pleasure and pressure was pushing me toward another orgasm. "Con, I'm going to–"

He laughed darkly when I couldn't bring myself to say it. "Go ahead, but I'm not done yet. I have more I want to do to you. Show you."

I lost count of how many times I orgasmed that night.

At some point, the lamp got knocked off the side table, plunging us into darkness. Finally, half on the couch, half on the floor, our bodies so slick with sweat that we nearly slid off each other, Con let himself come. I wrapped my arms around his neck, holding him tightly while he jerked and spasmed inside me.

"Fuck," he breathed, sinking down onto me, finally exhausted and spent. "Lily, you're going to kill me."

"Me?" I laughed, pushing at his shoulder. "You're the one with all the tricks."

He shifted his weight so that he was entirely on the couch, then pulled me against him. We were both breathing hard, damp with perspiration. There was a blanket on the floor, but neither of us reached for it.

"Con." I tilted my head back on his shoulder so that I could see his face. "This wasn't a mistake."

He didn't open his eyes, but he didn't deny it either.

"And if you ever try to send me away again–"

His eyes opened now, and his grip around me tightened. "You're not going anywhere, Lily."

Relief filled me.

"And if I ever see Devon's fucking face in the office again–"

I shook my head hard. "He's a nice guy."

Con's grip tightened further, warningly.

"But I was only using him to make you jealous," I confessed.

"It worked."

I smiled into his shoulder. "I know."

21

CON

I'd tried.

I didn't know if that counted for anything, but at least if I had to explain this to Halley one day, I could honestly say I'd tried. But all my efforts amounted to nothing. I couldn't put the genie back in the bottle. I stared down at Lily. Her naked body was only half covered by the soft blanket I'd pulled over us in the night. She was curled against me, her hair spilling over the arm I kept around her. She had one arm hooked around my chest. My shoulder was her pillow. I could feel her light breathing skittering across my clavicle. Her leg was draped over mine, golden against my paler skin. I pulled the blanket up higher, though I'd never seen anything as beautiful as the length of her body wrapped around mine.

The movement woke her. I felt her eyelashes flutter open before she raised her head to blink sleepily at me. "Good morning," she whispered.

"Good morning," I said.

We stared at each other as the sleep slowly faded from her eyes and a shadow of concern took its place. "Do you remember what you said?"

I nodded slowly.

"And you're not trying to take it back?" she demanded.

I shook my head. "No, I'm not trying to take it back. But–"

"No buts." Lily settled her head back on my shoulder. Her limbs tightened around me. "I'm not going anywhere."

I called Laura later that day to tell her Lily wasn't coming after all.

"You're in trouble, old pal," Laura said.

"You don't know the half of it," I said and hung up.

I hated myself for not having the strength to make her go, but after last night, I'd given up. Whatever had dragged us together was inexorable. The only thing to do now was to let it run its course and hope it let go before we completely fucked up each other's lives.

* * *

After that night, we began spending every free minute together that we could. I kept thinking that it would get old. I would get bored. We would have nothing in common. The age difference would widen between us like a canyon until we couldn't remember what the hell had brought us together in the first place.

But that never happened.

It wasn't just about the sex, though I was enjoying teaching Lily everything I knew. She was smart. Mature. We weren't as different as I had assumed. Granted, she hadn't had to grow up as fast as I did and raise a child while doing so, but she'd had to work harder than most of her peers to afford college. It bred in her the same sense of distance from her friends–even her best friends.

But we never mentioned Halley directly. Not to each other.

Not even when the topic of having children inexplicably came up. In retrospect, I couldn't remember how it had come up. Lily had been talking about where she wanted to live after law school–she was second guessing the big city now that she had had a taste of LA. It wasn't where she wanted to raise a family.

I stiffened. We never talked about the future like this. We were lying in bed, me propped up against the pillows, her curled up with her head on my thigh. I'd been stroking her hair, but now my hand stilled.

She rolled over to face me. "Could you see yourself having more kids?"

I jerked my shoulders noncommittally. It would have been easier if I could've said *hell no*, but the truth was, I didn't know. Maybe. I couldn't say that to Lily though–it would have opened up an avenue that neither of us was ready to go down. "I used to think about it," I said finally, "what it would be like if I'd met the right person and had a kid at the right time. Not when I was a kid myself, you know. When I wouldn't have to hustle so hard and could have enjoyed it more." Then I changed the subject.

Aside from these brushes with the future, Lily and I lived completely in the present. We had our own world. After we left the office, we went to my place. We didn't care that we spent all of our time in a two-thousand-square-foot box on top of the sky, not as long as I could touch her when-ever I wanted–however I wanted–without worrying that someone from The Walker Agency would see us. We ordered take out from all over the city. In addition to educating her about the various sex positions that existed, I was introducing her to the culinary delights the city had to offer. In her world, TGIFridays was a good meal. I was determined to change that.

"I don't want to get used to Sushi Zo though," she

protested, laughing, one night. "Because one day I'll go back to TGIFridays, and I won't be able to enjoy it."

"Good," I said, handing her chopsticks. "You shouldn't." But though we were both still smiling, something had dimmed between us. Lily had done what we tried never to do–talk about the future.

My friends were the only ones who knew about us–as far as I knew, Lily hadn't told anyone. Initially, they'd treated it like a joke. Increasingly, I saw them trade concerned glances when I left happy hour early to get back to her.

"It's getting pretty serious between you two," Garrett said as carefully as he could, which for a crisis manager, wasn't all that fucking careful. I knew exactly what he was getting at, and I had to fight to keep from scowling at him.

"Sex and takeout is serious now?" I asked, putting on an unconvincing smirk instead. I was trying to fool someone that this thing with Lily wasn't actually getting as serious as he seemed to think, even if it was only myself.

Four versions of skeptical expressions stared back at me. My friends could always see through me, and they took sadistic pleasure on calling me on my bullshit. Normally I appreciated it and returned the favor with equally sadistic pleasure. Today though, I felt my smirk drop into the scowl I'd tried to avoid.

"Fuck off," I said, signaling for the check.

"You want my opinion?" Garrett asked.

I knew it was a rhetorical question, but I answered anyway. "Hell no."

"You need to be honest," he went on as though he hadn't heard me. His gaze was unusually serious. He wasn't speaking as my buddy anymore; he was trying to avert a crisis. But there wasn't going to be one. Lily and I were too careful for that. We barely looked at each other in the office.

We staggered our arrivals and departures. It was almost ludicrous how cautious we were, because we knew we couldn't risk anyone from The Walker Agency seeing us. The silver lining was that the restraint we had to show all day exploded when we got each other alone. She was alone right now, in my apartment, and I was trapped here. I caught the server's eye again and frowned, making it clear I was ready to leave now.

Garrett was still talking, his voice low and intent. "You're playing with fire, Con. This thing is going to blow up in your face. It doesn't matter how careful you are. You think I don't know what I'm talking about? I make my fucking living on mistakes blowing up in people's faces. People who are a hell of a lot smarter than you."

Remembering his barstool swinging client, I doubted that they were that much smarter. "Thanks for the advice," I said levelly, handing off my credit card without even glancing at the bill.

Garrett scanned my face, then settled back in his barstool. "I'll invoice you," he said, resigned.

For the next week, I doubled down on being careful. Lily joked that we would have to start wearing disguises even in the apartment if I got any more paranoid. She said it with a laugh, but I caught the flash of wariness in her eyes before she busied herself with opening the wine.

"Hey," I grabbed her around the waist and turned her around. "Look at me."

She didn't want to, but she reluctantly turned her face up to mine. I studied the expression in her bottomless blue gaze. Was that hurt mixed in with the wariness? "What's wrong?"

Lily tried to look away, but I wouldn't let her. "Talk to me, Lily," I ordered, my voice hardening as my stomach tightened. She was getting sick of this shit, just like I knew she would. She was remembering that there was a city full of men who wouldn't have to lock her away in their penthouses to spend time together. She might even be thinking about that asshole Devon with his farm boy good looks. I had to find a reason to fire him.

"I'm just–" she bit her lip.

I braced myself, my brain already doing damage control. This would feel like shit, but ultimately, it was good. Necessary. Garrett was right. I had been playing with fire, and the match was burning low. If we kept up like this, both of us would go up in flames.

"--tired of feeling like your dirty little secret," Lily burst out. "I love–" she clamped down hard on the last word.

Now my stomach tensed for a different reason. If she said it, things would change between us. They'd have to. She'd be breaking the unspoken rules of whatever this thing between us was. I should have cut her off, found a way to change the subject, but instead, I waited. Did I *want* her to say it? It didn't make any fucking sense. If she did, I'd have to let her go. Wouldn't I?

"I love being with you," Lily redirected, her gaze flickering away for a moment before coming back to rest on mine earnestly. She slid her arms around my waist "I just wish it didn't have to be something we hid."

I pulled her in close, relief and something less tangible warring in my chest. I hadn't fucking wanted her to say it. I *hadn't*.

So why did I feel the same way I did when I walked away from a negotiation I hadn't killed at? What was that gnawing dissatisfaction and conviction that I'd left something on the table about? I had a beautiful woman who I actually enjoyed being with, aside from when we were having sex, and better yet, there was an expiration date.

So what the hell was wrong with me?

22

LILY

I was so wrapped up in what was happening with Con that the rest of my life faded into a blur. I knew money was stacking up in my savings account, but I wasn't doing a thing to prepare for law school otherwise, despite the stack of law books I'd brought with me to LA. Though Con had offered again to set me up with his friend Laura's firm, I'd resisted. It didn't matter that I couldn't so much as walk into the office with him, it was enough that I knew he was there. And sometimes, when Angie went to lunch, we threw off our usual caution for a few minutes.

I had some idea that this wasn't healthy, but I didn't care. I'd prioritized my future my entire life. Now I was completely intoxicated by my present, and I couldn't bring myself to look beyond it. For the first time, I was afraid of it. Not of law school–I knew that I could catch up–but of being without Con. It was October now, not that you'd know it by LA. Back in Ohio, the days would already be cold and gray. Here it was the land of perpetual summer, except that I always had a countdown in my head. We'd had one glorious month, but we only had eight left. It would pass in a flash, just like senior year had. And then...

My mind couldn't go beyond it. It was like trying to imagine infinity. I couldn't imagine an ending with Con anymore than I could imagine an endless universe. I focused on forgetting about time altogether–something that should have been easy enough to do in LA.

After our conversation about not wanting to be his secret, Con texted me an address.

"What's this?" I asked.

"A surprise. Meet me there at six tomorrow."

I tilted my head curiously, but he only smiled enigmatically. "Wear heels."

I wore the highest pair I owned, the pair I didn't dare wear out to a bar or club because I didn't know how long I'd be able to walk in them. They made my legs look as long and slim as a deer's, giving me the confidence to wear the flirty dress with the short hemline I'd bought recently. I'd been in the city for months, but when I saw myself in the mirror, for the first time I thought I looked like I belonged.

And when I got to the address he'd sent me, I felt like I was walking into another girl's life. It was a hole in the wall from the outside, but the inside reminded me of the restaurants Halley had taken me to when we were in Italy. Small places that you found off winding, cobblestone alleys behind unmarked doors with sheets of fresh pasta hanging in the windows.

Con was standing in the small waiting area with a reckless grin on his face. I felt myself light up at the sight of him, but I couldn't stop myself from scanning the dining room in search of a familiar face. There were none to be seen. Though the room wasn't big, the space was curated for intimacy. Small tables with chairs set close together sat apart from each other. The room was dim and mostly lit by ancient-looking brass chandeliers and long white tapers. It was filled with couples who only had eyes for each other.

It was safe.

We were seated at a round table in the corner covered in a white tablecloth. The taper already had fat waxy rolls down the side, pooling on the brass holder. Con's eyes glowed with satisfaction as he stared at me over it. "This is Giardo's. It's my favorite place in the city. I've wanted to bring you here for a while."

"I'm glad you did." A smile spread across my face as I looked into his. I was barely aware of what we were saying aloud to each other. There was something humming beneath the words. I hadn't even had a sip of the deep, purplish-red claret decanting at the edge of the table, but I felt intoxicated by the place, and more immediately, by the man.

The waiter who brought a basket of fresh, hot bread with crispy edges and a soft, sunken center knew Con by name and asked if he wanted his usual. Then he winked at me and said, "Finally, he brings a lady."

I laughed. "That's smooth."

He raised his eyebrows questioningly. "What is?"

"The line—it is a line, isn't it?" I looked at Con. "I'm not—"

His face was unreadable, impenetrable. "You are."

After the server walked away, I stared at him. "This is your favorite place in the city, and you've never brought anyone here before?"

He moved his large shoulders. "I never wanted to before."

The glow that had kindled in me when I first walked in grew brighter, filled me to the brim with warm, golden light. The words *I love you* threatened to burble up and spill over my lips. I didn't want to swallow them back. It didn't feel natural to repress what was becoming more and more true every day. But I couldn't risk it. Saying *I love you* would draw a line in the sand that neither of us would know whether we should cross or not.

Instead, I tried to keep it light. I rubbed the pointed toe of my heel against the inside of his leg and said teasingly, "I guess you could say I'm *your* first."

As I knew they would, his eyes darkened, and his body leaned toward mine instinctively. Dinner at Giardo's was like delicious, exquisitely and painfully drawn-out foreplay. It was a place to linger. We dipped the bread in rich, peppery olive oil and drank wine for the first hour, not putting in our orders until it was nearly 8:30. When the entrees arrived, we ate languidly, sharing bites of his carbonara and my fettuccine until the plates were empty. I didn't think I could possibly eat dessert, but Con insisted on ordering the tiramisu. By the time we finished the last bite and drank our after-dinner digestive, a colorless liqueur that tasted like black licorice—it was nearly eleven.

Emboldened by getting away with having dinner together in public, Con and I walked hand in hand to his car. We left mine parked in the lot and he drove us back to his place without even having to discuss it. There was no need to go back to mine anymore. Dinner had changed us. Maybe it would only be for the night, but I had a feeling this deepness, this *connection*, would last. We didn't even wait until the elevator got us up to his penthouse before we were on each other. Kissing, touching, pulling each other deeper and closer than we'd ever been. If the ride had been longer, who knew what we would have done in the ornate cubicle. I might have thrown caution to the wind and told him I loved him. For some reason, that seemed possible now. Less like a death sentence anyway.

We broke apart before the elevator doors slid open, but our hands were still loosely clasped, still standing so closely together that our arms brushed. Hazy with wine and lust, we stepped out into his private lobby.

And froze.

There was a pair of shoes kicked off in the corner. Low white tennis shoes with double-knotted laces, frayed and graying from chronic use. The kind Halley always wore around campus.

I froze, sobriety slamming into me like a Mack truck. Halley. The long weekend. What day was it? She wasn't supposed to be here until–

It was Thursday. She'd flown out after her afternoon class because she didn't have any on Friday. She'd landed at LAX at six–right when I was walking into Giardo's.

I hadn't looked at my phone all night. I probably had a dozen missed calls and messages, wondering where I was.

"Oh my God," I whispered.

Con had gone white as a sheet. Whiter than those shoes had ever been. He dropped my hand like it had caught fire. A chasm opened between us instantly.

"Dad, is that you?" Halley's voice called from the kitchen. We had only moments before she came around the corner and saw us.

Instinctively, I stumbled back into the elevator. I caught a glimpse of Con's eyes, wild and dark, before the doors slid closed. I jabbed the Lobby button desperately, terrified that the doors would slide back open for some reason and Halley would see me. There would be no covering this up if she did. My hair was disheveled from the ride up and I was wearing *fuck me* heels the likes of which she'd never seen on me.

If the ride up had been heaven, the ride back down was hell. As soon as the relief of escaping faded, a wretched shame took its place.

What was I doing, running away from the man I loved

and hiding from my best friend? I'd only done the requisite Psych 101 course my freshman year, but even I knew those two things meant there was something fundamentally wrong. There was no exception to the rule.

I walked down the block to the safety and loneliness of my building. I couldn't remember the last time I'd spent a night here alone. Even in my wretched state, I felt lucky that Con and I spent most of his time at his place. If Halley had walked in on us in her condo...

Chills raced through me. I let myself into the condo and leaned back against the closed door. Down the hallway, I could see the back of the pink couch. The edge of the island in the kitchen. Places Con and I had made love. We'd gotten very lucky that we'd happened to go out tonight.

How long would our luck hold?

How long could we keep hiding?

How long would I still want to?

23

CON

Halley's visit was excruciating for a number of reasons.

One, I'd never needed to lie to my daughter before. Now it was all I was doing. Answers to simple questions had to be lies.

Where were you out so late, dressed so nice?

Work shit.

What actress is trying to become my stepmother this week?

No one special.

Don't you love Lily?

She's fine.

Her visit also made it so I couldn't see Lily for three days. Not really see her, anyway. I had to settle for staring at the back of her head on Friday instead of focusing on the contract I was negotiating. Friday night and all of Saturday were shitty, empty hours because I was used to filling them with Lily. Then there was the truly brutal Sunday night when all three of us went out to dinner. I hadn't seen her since she left work on Friday, but I couldn't really look at her now. Not the way I wanted to. It was like laying out an all-you-can-eat buffet in front of a starving man and telling him *not yet*.

We went to Halley's favorite steak house, the one I'd taken Lily to the first time for lunch. Our gazes crossed briefly, both of us silently acknowledging the connection. A soft smile tugged at her lips. It went downhill from there. Halley and Lily sat on the same side of the table while I sat across from them. I heard myself saying banal shit like, *Order whatever you want. It's on me.*

Halley gave me a funny look because of course it was on me. I was the dad, after all.

Lily looked miserably uncomfortable, but she tried to cover it up for Halley's sake. The two of them fell back on conversations about people they knew from college that I had zero interest in. I ordered a second beer and tried not to let my gaze linger on Lily too long. I missed her. I missed the physicality of her in my space, in my bed. The halo of sunshine her hair created in my peripheral vision. The warmth of her legs tangled in mine. It wasn't just about sex though. I could have gotten that somewhere else. It was galling to realize, but I was fucking lonely without her. Not once in the last three years since Halley left college had I missed having someone in the house. I'd always been a loner who never got a chance to be alone. Now the emptiness of the penthouse mocked me. I wanted to order food with her, bitch about my latest negotiation to her. I wanted to celebrate how I'd finally gotten Sienna Birch signed onto a career making movie. I even wanted to listen to her talk about her day, and that was a new feeling.

But I couldn't, because Lily wasn't in my penthouse where she belonged. She and Halley were out hitting the nightspots or curled up on that pink couch watching movies and doing face masks or some shit. I imagined she was having to lie a lot too. I bet she liked it about as much as I

164

did. Neither of us were liars. I'd never cared enough to deceive someone, and Lily was too honest.

The only thing that rescued the miserable dinner was the knowledge that it was Halley's last night in town. I was going to drive her to LAX tomorrow after my morning meeting with my lawyer. Lily and I would have another four weeks or so before Halley came back for Thanksgiving. I half hoped that by then, whatever this thing was between us had run its course. As shitty as it was to miss Lily, it was just as shitty to wish my daughter back across the country.

Lily and Halley were going out for Halley's last night. Halley had someone she wanted Lily to meet. Lily avoided both of our eyes and said she didn't want to meet anyone.

"Still all work and no play?" Halley clicked her tongue, exasperated. "Dad, tell Lily she can't work her youth away."

"I actually highly recommend it," I said, grateful that they had decided they didn't want dessert and that we could finally end this sham. "That's what I did."

Lily's eyes flickered up to mine, amusement in the blue depths. Halley rolled hers. "And look at you now. Going home alone to your plants every night."

"Haven't you hated every girlfriend he's ever had?" Lily asked, her eyes back on the table.

Halley elbowed her. "Well, yeah, but I had reasons."

Lily and I both paused, waiting for her to go on. Halley had already lost interest though. She was texting, her thumbs flying furiously across the keyboard. Lily's gaze brushed across mine again. I felt it like a physical touch. The expression in her eyes was so clear I could read her mind.

By this time tomorrow, we were both thinking.

After we left the restaurant, Lily and Halley's plans had them going the opposite direction I was heading.

"I'll see you tomorrow, Dad," Halley said, giving me a quick hug goodbye. "Call me when you're outside."

"I will. And I'll see *you* bright and early tomorrow," I said to Lily, careful not to look her in the eye. I knew Halley would take the comment as the directive of a boss to an employee and not what it really was.

My daughter groaned dramatically. "Come on, Dad. Let Lily live a little."

"I don't want to live a little," Lily said, and then looking at me, "I'll be there."

The exchange was brief, but it felt so intimate and loaded that I couldn't believe Halley didn't look back and forth between us suspiciously.

But she didn't, and I walked away feeling better than I had in days. This fucking interminable dinner was over, and I would get Lily back tomorrow. I hadn't gotten a chance to get her alone since she threw herself back into the elevator, just saving us from having to make some extremely unpleasant explanations to Halley. The look on her face as the elevator doors closed had haunted me though. Her eyes had been wide with shock and fear, but there had been pain in them, too. In that moment, it had hit me again how wrong I was for her, and how unfair that was to her. Over the last three days, I'd tortured myself with thinking about how many men in this city could treat her the way she deserved. And then I'd thought about how I'd maim every last one of them if they so much as looked at her.

Now, though, I knew she wasn't thinking about them. She was promising me things with her eyes that I'd collect on later—this time tomorrow in fact.

* * *

As it turned out, I wasn't able to see Lily come into the office bright and early. My lawyer, Jones, asked if I could meet earlier, and then he confirmed what I'd suspected. Kim's counsel was reaching out, probing for more money. First, she'd claimed that she'd paid expenses for Halley's education that I needed to reimburse her for half of. Everything she brought up was bullshit. I'd paid 100% of tuition, room, board, and books. I'd paid for the summer immersion trips. I'd even covered the sorority fees even though I didn't get why the hell she wanted to join one. Kim must have known that wouldn't work, because she also offered up a cleverly worded NDA. If I paid her enough, she'd never say another word about me. Not to the press, not to gossip bloggers, not even to her cat.

"I think that's blackmail," I said to Jones.

He shrugged as if that was just semantics. "She thinks she could get a book deal."

I snorted in disbelief. "You've got to be fucking with me. I'm the head of a talent agency, not George Clooney."

"You'd be surprised," Jones said seriously. "She can create a good angle. Claim to have been in the inner circle throughout the Me Too movement. Juxtapose that with her experience co-parenting a child with you, a powerful man. How your stature affected the dynamic, how inequitable the court system can be—"

"You mean how it favors mothers?" I demanded. Twenty years ago, I'd been through hell and back trying to get full custody of Halley. It didn't matter how much dumb shit Kim did. How many times she drove under the influence or disturbed the peace. The court kept trying to give my daughter back to her. Halley had been seven before I was finally awarded full physical and legal custody and Kim was reduced to supervised visits.

"I mean how it favors money," Jones said, unruffled. "Now I'm not saying that was the case, but it could play well in a book. People are just going to see that your dad owned the agency–"

"He owned a small agency with seven clients and turned a profit that barely covered the overhead," I corrected.

"Doesn't matter what it was. It was *called* The Walker Agency, same as it is now. If Kim wants to, she's going to make you look like an asshole who was handed everything and used his daddy's money to take custody away from a loving mother." Jones spread his hands out in apology. "I'm not telling you what to do. I'm just telling you what I think she can make it look like."

It pissed me off to know Jones was right. "What would you do?" I asked grudgingly.

"I can't tell you that."

"Come on, Jones. Not as my lawyer, just as a friend. Would you pay her?"

Jones paused, then nodded. "Yeah, I would."

On my way to pick up Halley, I called Garrett to talk about it. He agreed with Jones. "You can do damage control, but you know what I always say about damage control."

"It's an oxymoron. Once you've taken damage, you've lost control." I rubbed my eyes and glared at all the red brake lights in front of me. "The only real damage control is to avoid the hit all together."

"That's right," Garrett said. "Glad someone listens to me."

"So you think I should pay her too?"

I couldn't see him over the phone, but I could practically hear his careless shrug in his tone of voice. "I don't know. I honestly can't see it making much of a dent in your career. It's not ugly enough."

"It would be ugly for Halley though." Frustrated, I thumped my fist on the driver's side window. The passenger in the car next to me looked over. "You think that has any chance of stopping Kim?"

"Halley's feelings?" Garrett sounded droll. "No. I don't."

"Yeah, me either," I sighed. "I'll pay."

"Look at the bright side," Garrett said. "At least she doesn't have the PI tailing you anymore."

"Some bright side," I said, and hung up. The real bright side would be when Halley was safely at LAX and I could get back to Lily.

24

LILY

As soon as Con picked Halley up for the airport midday on Monday, I went to his penthouse. It was disturbingly like coming home. I walked around, checking on the plants. Greeting them like old friends. I walked into his bedroom and felt a wave of anticipation roll over me. Soon. Soon.

When he finally walked through the door, I couldn't stop myself from throwing myself into his arms.

He caught me deftly and hoisted me up in his arms. I wrapped my legs around his waist, my arms around his neck, and sank against him. It felt so good to be pressed against him like this. A relief, a release that went beyond sex. I loved him.

"I missed you," I said later, when we were lying in bed naked.

"I missed you too." He was rubbing his thumb idly over my nipple, and it was starting to make me wet all over again. "It was hell sitting across from you and not being able to touch you."

"Do you think we'll ever be able to tell her?" I wondered.

We were both quiet for a moment, unable to picture it. "I don't know," Con said finally. "It's starting to feel shittier and shittier to lie to her."

"Maybe we're overthinking it. Maybe it wouldn't be such a big deal."

Con snorted. I didn't bother pursuing that fantasy any further. We both knew it would be a huge deal to Halley. I ran my fingers through his hair while he continued to stroke my breasts. "You know what's funny?" I asked, then clamped my lips shut. "Never mind."

Con raised his head, his dark eyes intent on mine. "Tell me."

"It's not *funny*," I temporized. "It's...I don't know. Interesting, I guess."

He waited.

"You can't tell her I told you, but Halley has a secret she keeps from you, too."

"I don't want to hear about my daughter's love life, Lily," he said warningly.

"No. It's about her career. She wants to be an actress, and she's terrified to tell you. Just like you're afraid to tell her about me."

Con stared at me. "Halley wants to be an actress?"

I nodded. "It's all she's ever wanted to do. She said you told her she had to go to college, no matter what. She was afraid if she tried to go in LA, the temptation to join the industry would be too much. But once she graduates, that's her plan."

Con shook his head, his mouth thinning. "I hate it, but there's nothing I can do about it. She went to college like I asked."

"Do you think there's any scenario in which you tell her about me, and she doesn't like it but accepts it?"

Neither of us could answer that question, so we pushed

it away. It felt too good to be together again to let anything ruin it. We fell back into our old pattern of spending every minute together that we could and acting like polite near strangers at work. We still had sex every chance we got and ordered food from all over the city, but things were deepening between us, too. He even opened up about what was going on with Halley's mother.

"You gave her a million dollars to sign an NDA?" I gasped.

"I'd give her twice that to go the fuck away," Con said grimly, "but she cares about Halley *just* enough not to take it."

I'd met Kim a few times. She was beautiful and terrible. Halley couldn't see it, but I did. She loved Halley like her daughter was a commodity. A designer purse. A luxury vacation. I shivered with anger, thinking about how casually she was willing to hurt Halley. No wonder Con went to such lengths to protect her.

"At least she signed it," I said. "And once Halley graduates, she's out of your life, right?"

"She's out of my wallet anyway, and that's all I care about."

Though Con didn't show a flicker of emotion, I felt wild, defensive anger on his behalf. I kissed him gently and loved him more tenderly than ever before. I wanted to protect him from things that had already happened. Kim. This city. Himself.

At night, when he fell asleep, I whispered what he wasn't ready to hear when he was awake. *I love you.* His slow, steady breathing never changed.

* * *

Early one Tuesday morning, I woke up with my mouth watering. It wasn't from hunger. My stomach was roiling, and I could already feel vomit climbing up my esophagus. I barely made it to the bathroom before I threw up. Then I sagged against the porcelain toilet.

"Oh, don't," I moaned when Con appeared in the doorway, his eyes heavy with sleep, the lower half of his face shadowed with stubble. Looking way too good to see me looking my worst.

Ignoring my protestations, he crossed the tile to the sink and wet a washcloth. Squatting down beside me, he pressed it to my forehead. The cool water sank into my hairline, drip dropped down my cheeks, but it made me feel better. No less embarrassed, but better.

"Do you think it was the fish?" he asked with a frown.

I shrugged weakly. "Maybe, but we had the same thing."

When I was sure I wasn't going to throw up again, he helped me back to bed. "I'll tell Angie you called out sick," he said, pulling the covers up around me. "Stay home today. Feel better."

Home. I wondered if he had any idea how many directions that one word sent my mind spinning off into. I'd barely been back to Halley's condo in the last few weeks, but I was still careful not to call the penthouse *home.* The idea of it made me feel warm inside though. Coming *home* to Con at the end of every day.

While he showered and got ready for work, I curled up with the idea. Built it up. Luxuriated in the fantasy of it. By the time he was ready to go, the nausea that had sunk into my guts like a fishhook and dragged me to the toilet was a distant memory.

"I feel like I could go to work," I said. "I'll just be a little late."

Con leaned over the bed, pushing me back gently against the pillows. "Take a day, Lily. I have happy hour after work with the guys, but I'll leave early."

After he left, I padded happily around the penthouse wearing the t-shirt he'd slept in. It smelled like him and was so big on me it was like a sleep shirt. After I ate and was sure the nausea wasn't going to make a triumphant return, I called my mom. I hadn't talked to her in a while.

"Hi stranger," she said when she picked up. Her voice was filled with delight and not a hint of recrimination for how long it had been. "Shouldn't you be at work?"

I glanced at the clock. Too early for a lunch hour. "I'm taking a sick day. It was the weirdest thing. I woke up sick, threw up, and then felt fine."

"That does sound weird," she agreed. "Maybe you're pregnant." She laughed when she said it, so sure it wasn't even a remote possibility. She knew I'd never slept with any of the serious boyfriends I'd had in college, and I hadn't even told her I was seeing someone in the city.

While she laughed, my blood ran cold, then a hot flush rose into my cheeks. The breath evaporated from my lungs, leaving me gasping. I couldn't have faked a laugh if I'd wanted to.

"Lily? Are you there?" her voice sobered. "I was just kidding, honey. I know you're waiting for the right one."

She was worried she'd offended me. I managed to draw in enough air to reassure her. "Sorry, mom. I'm just—I'm feeling sick again. Can I call you back?"

After we hung up, I threw on a pair of jeans and wore Con's t-shirt to the pharmacy down the street. I bought a pack of condoms and a two-pack of pregnancy tests and was grateful that the cashier didn't have anything funny to say about it.

Then I raced back to the penthouse, my heart beating wildly. My whole life might be about to change, and I had no idea how I felt about it.

25

CON

From an outsider's perspective, I'd been on top of the world for a long time now. I'd accomplished everything I set out to do when I was a scared shitless nineteen-year-old kid who felt like he had *one* shot to make a life for his infant daughter. My name was synonymous with success. It opened doors for talent I believed in and people I cared about. My infant daughter was now on the precipice of being a college graduate and being able to do anything. I had more money than I could spend and more houses than I could live in. I even had real friends, something that was harder to come by than success in this town. In fact, the two rarely coexisted. I'd known abstractly that I had plenty of reasons to feel cocky, but a small part of me always felt like I was putting on a show. The slick, successful hot shot with the five-thousand-dollar suit and thirty-thousand dollar smile and everything else that was designed to distract from what was underneath. Secretly, it had all felt like a giant sleight of hand. A lifelong game of misdirection. I had everything, and yet I'd always felt like something was missing. I was never sure what it was. I chalked it up to uncertainty. Told myself it would go away when I had a certain amount of money in the bank, a certain number of Oscar winners in my roster. When Halley got through those god-awful middle school years. When she got out of those sly, secretive high school years.

And at each milestone, I'd waited for the feeling to go away.

It never had.

As I waited for my friends at our favorite rooftop bar, my mind slid to it absently. Probed for it. And felt an electric current ripple all the way through my body as I realized it was gone. The dull ache, the vague frustration that came with it, the renewed determination to achieve *more*. It was all gone. Instead, I felt...

I frowned, trying to figure out what it was.

Relaxed?

No, that wasn't it. The furrows in my forehead lengthened, and my frown deepened as I tried to put a name to the sensation.

Calm?

"You look pissed," Landon observed, sliding into the barstool across from mine.

"I'm not," I said, still frowning.

"Is he acting?" Garrett wondered.

Dominic and Julian snorted. They began imagining what role I might be preparing an audition for. I heard the names *Heathcliff* and *Dracula* thrown out.

"If that's not your pissed off face, what is it?" Landon asked.

"Peace," I said, finding the word suddenly. That was what I felt. Fucking *peace*. Like I'd just finished a ninety-minute hot yoga session after an ayahuasca ceremony followed by tree bathing or whatever new age shit promised to bring about peace these days.

"If that's how you look when you feel peaceful, I'd hate

to see you pissed," Garrett said, raising his eyebrows in surprise.

I didn't bother trying to explain further. They didn't get it. They weren't in love. The realization that I loved Lily bloomed, fully formed in my head, before my mind could yank it out by its roots. I pictured her heart-shaped face with the ocean blue eyes and the innocent beauty of a girl fresh out of college sprung into my mind in full, detailed, Technicolor.

Fuck. I really did love her.

While their conversation moved on, ebbing and flowing around me, I drank my beer and thought about Lily. The more I thought about her, the more the feeling intensified. I could lie by omission to the others, but I couldn't deceive myself. For some fucked up reason, my mind had decided that *Lily* was the missing piece. Not any of the accomplished career women I'd dated over the years. Not any of the society women I'd been set up with now and then. Not any of the actresses who had made it all too clear what they were willing to do to get signed to The Walker Agency.

A twenty-three-year-old who happened to be my daughter's best friend.

If I hadn't been feeling so damn peaceful, I might have groaned out loud. Of all the fucked-up things to do to a man, the universe had really outdone itself with this one.

I pushed my empty pint glass away and shook my head when the bartender asked if I wanted another. I needed a clear head to figure out what the hell I was going to do. How I was going to get out of this without tanking my reputation, alienating my daughter, and generally ruining my fucking life.

I had to stop. The next steps played out in my mind. Telling her. Dealing with whatever emotions she threw at me. I'd deserve any of them. It made my guts clench, remembering that she had been a virgin before I came along. And when the storm had passed, and she had moved on...what then? That was where I stopped being able to visualize the next step. It was a slate gray wall that my mind refused to look beyond. Me, who had had a twenty-year plan since he was nineteen years old.

Frustrated, I tried another play. What if we just fucking went for it? Told everyone. Made it public. I'd find her another position—maybe one in an entertainment law firm. It would look shady as fuck if we were caught, but what if I just took her to the next big premiere? A couple of tongues would wag, but that was all. A few pithy comments, maybe a few nasty blind items on Perez Hilton with comments from Brand Development people thinly disguised as anonymous sources.

Yeah, that could work.

But then there was Halley.

My heart sank, and the peace shrank back as I pictured my daughter's face screwed up in disgust as the realization that I was fucking her best friend. Because that might be all she could see, no matter how hard I tried to dress it up.

I was trapped between the two people who meant the most to me in the world, and the thing of it was, Lily had no right to be as important to me as Halley. I ground my teeth, trying to remind myself that Lily was not as important to me as my daughter.

Except she was, and I loved her.

"Is this your peaceful face again?" Garrett asked, pausing mid-sentence to study me with mock concern.

"Yes," I growled.

When they laughed, I decided it was time for me to go. I could figure this out in my apartment where I could think more clearly. My plants never interrupted with stupid fucking questions or observations, and that was just one of the many reasons why they were better than people.

I nodded brusquely to the PI who had reappeared. He was sitting at the bar with a water, squeezing a second lemon into it. When he saw me, he jerked his head in the universal *come here* gesture.

I paused and glanced around, sure he must be talking to someone else. This wasn't how we played this game. But now he was drying lemon juice off his fingers with a cocktail napkin and then holding up his hand, halfway between looking like a mob boss beckoning over a minion and a student half-heartedly raising his hand to answer a question.

I made my way over, trying not to show my surprise. He was probably going to ask me to buy him another drink, or maybe get him out of some of the parking tickets I knew he was collecting. He was getting too familiar, I decided. Son of a bitch would probably expect to be invited to The Walker Agency holiday party.

Up close, he looked like a basset hound. Droopy eyes, long face, cheeks that seemed to fold down from his hollow eye sockets. Friendly though, and a little sheepish. Again, I wondered what he was going to ask me for.

"Hey boss," he said.

I realized it was the first time I'd heard his voice. Low, gravelly, like he'd spent a few years gargling rocks. But, like his face, friendly.

"I'm the boss, huh." I slid into the stool beside him. I wasn't sure why I was sitting down. If he'd asked me for something, I'd have refused by now and been on my way to the door. But he hadn't asked, and he was looking at me with those sympathetic, droopy brown eyes, like *I* was the dog, and he had to put me down.

"You jump, I jump," he said. "I'd say that makes you the boss."

"I haven't seen you around as much lately," I said. "I thought maybe Kim had gotten tired of paying you guys for nothing."

"She did. But then there started being something." His voice was still rough around the edges, but there was an apologetic note underlining the gravelly tones. I was starting to get a bad feeling about where this conversation was headed.

"Something," I repeated. "Something like what?"

He looked down at the lemon rinds floating in his water, his mouth tugging down. "Come on, boss. You know what."

I'd always prided myself on my ability to read people, but now I prayed that that was all bullshit, that I was as perceptive as a fence post. Because what I was reading in the sideways glance he sent me was that he knew all about Lily. Which meant Kim was going to know all about Lily. Which meant...

My stomach turned. The peace I'd felt only minutes ago turned inside out. Kim had signed the NDA in exchange for the final payment, but this wasn't information she'd take to the press or put in a book. It was information she'd pour into Halley's ear like poison.

I had a few hands to play now. First, I bluffed. "I don't know what you're talking about."

He sighed, and his breath skidded across the bar. "The girl, man. The blonde. Your daughter's pal. The one you took to Giardo's."

"Lily?" I tried to laugh. "That's just my daughter's friend."

He winced, like he was embarrassed for me. "There are pictures. The two of you leaving a club together, pulling her into the dark doorway. Leaving Giardo's hand in hand. More than I can count of her getting on your private elevator after work and leaving in the morning. An interesting one of her this morning wearing what I'm guessing is your shirt."

Pictures he'd taken, I was sure, but he was careful not to include that part. I felt, strangely, like he felt enormously guilty for what he was doing. Which gave me hope that the next hand I laid down would end the game.

"It isn't what it looks like," I said quietly. "It was just a few times."

Another sideways glance that told me the lie hadn't worked. "There's also a woman named Victoria. Claims Lily told her everything."

I was sure that was a lie. Kim had set this up somehow, but damned if I knew how. Although I guessed I'd made it pretty fucking easy once I let my guard down. "You were there all along," I said.

"Just doing my job." But his gaze fell from mine.

"Why now? You've had these pictures for a while."

He shrugged. "She owed me some money. She finally settled up."

She'd settled up with the fucking lump sum I'd given her in exchange for the NDA.

"If you give this to Kim, it's going to destroy my daughter," I said, my voice even lower. "Do you have kids?"

"Yeah, I do," he said, and then with a little wince of sympathy. "But I don't fuck their friends, so I can't say I know exactly how you're feeling."

He didn't serve the words with any particular malice, just fact. I had a feeling he'd admit to any manner of fuck-ups, but in this, his hands were clean and mine were dirty, and those were just the facts. I only had one more hand. "I'll pay you," I said, my voice so quiet that his eyes flickered up to mine questioningly. I repeated it. "I'll pay you. Whatever you ask."

The man was wearing sneakers that had to be older than Halley. It didn't look like he'd had a decent haircut this decade. Not to be an asshole, but I thought that was my trump card. I'd give him a hundred thousand dollars, and he'd tell Kim I was a choir boy.

So when he shook his head, I was dumbfounded.

"What's she paying you?" I pressed. "I'll double it. Fuck, I'll triple it. You know I'm good for it. You've seen where I live."

If circumstances had been any less serious, I'd have hated myself for the words coming out of my mouth. But they were serious. And I was willing to do anything.

He smiled a little, that half-embarrassed smile, like even he thought I was making an ass of myself. "Yeah, boss. I've seen where you live. Listen though, that has nothing to do with this or that. I'm contracted, and that's all there is to it. I just wanted to give you fair warning of what was coming. Give you a chance to, you know..." he spun his straw in his water.

"Spin it?" I guessed, watching the liquid swirl. It reminded me of the water in the toilet going down the drain, which was an apt metaphor for what was happening to my life right now.

"That's it," he said. He looked like he wanted to reach over and pat me reassuringly on the back, but he thought better of it. He stood, pulled a few dollar bills out of his pocket to leave on the bar, and left.

Taking any hope I had of getting out of this unscathed with him.

26

LILY

I should have been terrified, but instead, I felt a deluge of joy sweep through me. My rational, logical side tried to temper it.

What do you have to be happy about? You're barely twenty-three. You haven't even started law school. You're going to raise a baby while building your career? That'll be...interesting.

Funny, I'd never realized how snide my logical inner voice could sound. I answered it defensively. *Yes, it* will *be interesting. And amazing. Con did it when he was only nineteen, and so can I. Besides, I won't be doing it alone.*

Would I?

A whisper of trepidation cut through the argument I was having with myself. When I saw the positive sign on the pregnancy test, I also saw the future. Con standing in my hospital room, a bundled blanket in his arms. A sweet, peaceful profile peeking out from the folds, eyes closed, lashes resting against soft cheeks. I saw as if in a montage the blur of sleepless nights we'd get through together. The way he'd have to lean far over to hold the small grasping hands. I saw a dozen different scenes just like this, and it wasn't until now that I realized I wasn't just imagining them. I'd seen these pictures.

Con holding newborn Halley, looking so young and yet still somehow so confident. His tall body doubled over to hold both of her hands when she was learning to walk, twisting his neck to smile up at the camera. Not much older now, but with exhausted eyes. And on and on, until the most recent one she had of the two of them at her high school graduation.

Halley.

She would be the baby's big sister. I choked out a queer laugh at the realization. Now a new flood of images filled my mind. Con and I telling her together, our hands locked. A united front against the person we loved best. Con flying east to tell her without me while I waited in LA for the inevitable angry phone call. She'd get over it, I told myself. When she saw that I really loved him and this wasn't about his money or his power. When she saw how happy we were. She'd forgive us.

I couldn't quite conjure up that image though, so I pushed it all out of my mind. I couldn't deal with it now. I didn't want to. I wanted to feel that overwhelming joy again without the complications of real life. I curled up in a corner of the couch and wrapped my arms around the throw pillow, buried my face in it and imagined I was breathing in the scent of a newborn instead of wiry cotton fibers that smelled vaguely of my shampoo with the faintest hint of Con's aftershave. It reminded me of what we'd done on this couch to create the newborn I was imagining, and even with my face buried in the pillow, a blush rose to my cheeks. At the same time, my excitement surged again. I couldn't wait to tell him. He'd be surprised, but he said he'd thought about having more children. That he wished he had been able to do it with the right person and not have to spend their childhood scrambling and hustling.

He'd said it regretfully, like that chance had come and gone, but he was wrong. It was here.

I sprung to my feet and began pacing, my eyes sweeping the space. It was too small to raise a baby in. We could move into the Hills where he raised Lily, or maybe he'd even be willing to leave LA, if he was going to take a step back from his career anyway. A thrill shot through me as I pictured us raising our child in the palatial ski lodge he owned in Colorado or even the beach house in Croatia. Colorado would be better, I decided. I could do law school more easily if we stayed in the country. But nothing was impossible. Nothing at all.

I swept my hands up over my head and spun around, exhilarated. We could do anything now. He'd said it himself —he'd already achieved everything he ever wanted to in his career. Now we could live the life he'd thought had passed him by, and I would figure out how to build mine wherever that took us.

I ran lightly across the floor to the elevator bank, hoping to see the light that indicated he was coming up. Logically, I knew he was at happy hour with Landon, Garrett, Dominic, and Julian, but I still hoped that somehow, my boundless joy had crossed the distance between us and summoned him. I'd go to him, I decided. The guys knew anyway. But even before I pressed the button to summon the elevator, I changed my mind. No, that wasn't how I wanted to tell him.

It had to be special.

* * *

An hour and a half later, I was back in Con's apartment with takeaway from Giardo's. I'd also stopped at Candle Delirium on my way and picked up a few for the outdoor table. I'd picked up flowers from the Flower Market that I'd arranged in bunches in two beer steins—the closest thing I could find to a vase in his apartment. His carbonara was neatly plated on one side of the table, and my fettuccine was on the other. I'd put the bread in a small basket, and the hard butter pats were softening in the sun. The tiramisu was still in the refrigerator, but then I'd thought to Google it and found about a dozen articles claiming it was unsafe for pregnant women. I found a few that claimed it was, but I was going to play it safe. The dessert would just be for him, as would the bottle of red wine I had breathing in the kitchen.

I had texted him as soon as I got back, asking when he would be back. To my surprise, he still hadn't answered. I called once, but it went straight to voicemail. I worried a path between the elevator and the food, wondering if I should take it back in. But no, he *had* to be back soon. He'd said seven at the latest, and it was nearly eight.

At eight-thirty, I sat down in front of my fettuccine and twirled a bite onto my fork. I knew I should be hungry—I hadn't eaten since lunch at one—but the delicious sauce could have been dust for all I tasted it, and the noodles felt slimy and unappetizing. After only a bite, I set my fork down. A pit was opening up in my stomach. Why was he so late? Why hadn't he answered my text? Why was his phone off?

I reached for a piece of bread, thinking it might settle my stomach. By nine, I'd only taken a single bite, then shredded the rest into grain-sized pieces over my pasta.

Something was very, very wrong. He should have been home hours ago. I had to call someone—but who? I couldn't very well call Angie to see if Con had checked in. I couldn't ask Halley if she'd heard from him. I didn't have his friends' phone numbers. It would be crazy to start calling hospitals. The police were completely out of the question.

I unlocked my phone at least a dozen times, feeling the need to take action. Any action. But I couldn't think of a single thing to do. Suddenly, the isolation of our romance wasn't sexy and thrilling anymore. If this had been any other romantic partner, I'd have had scores of people to call. Mutual friends to start with. Mothers if I had to. And it wouldn't have been strange, because of course a girlfriend worried when her boyfriend didn't come home.

But Con wasn't my boyfriend.

He was somehow more and less. More to me—infinitely more. But to the world, he was nothing but my boss. The father of my best friend. Certainly not someone I should be worrying about after office hours.

We'd have to change that. The baby had already made it a certainty, but now I didn't want until twelve weeks or whenever it was safe to announce a pregnancy. I wanted the whole world to know that I had a claim on Con. That his wellbeing was mine to worry over. If he was still mine. I bit down on the inside of my lip, trying to stem the rising panic.

He was fine. Of course he was fine.

Any second now, I'd—

Like an answered prayer, I heard the quiet chime of the elevator carriage locking into place and the gentle woosh of the door sliding open. I pushed away from the table and met him as he was walking into the kitchen. It was on the tip of my tongue to cry *where have you been?* But even in my head, it sounded like a disgruntled wife. I swallowed it. "I was worried about you," I said instead.

Relief had started pumping through my veins, driving out the fear and making my feel tingly and lightheaded. Now that I got a good look at his face though, I froze. Con was home, but there was still something very, very wrong. His face was like a mask. When he looked at me, his eyes were those of a stranger.

"You don't need to worry about me," the stranger's voice said.

I peered closer at him, like a child trying to see if there was a man inside the Easter Bunny costume. "Con, what's wrong?" I asked. Instinctively, I tucked an arm over my stomach as if the tiny life inside needed protecting. But that was crazy. This was *Con*.

But Con would have noticed the wine breathing on the counter and the candles flickering outside, bright against the bruising twilight, and asked, "What's all this?" The stranger's eyes moved over the scene—and me—without interest. "What are you doing here?"

"What am I—" I floundered. "We were going to have dinner together, I thought."

"Were we? I forgot."

His voice was completely devoid of emotion. Anger lit inside me. Surely, he had to see that I'd gone to some trouble. Surely, he knew he was two hours later than he'd said he'd be. And surely, he knew that I would worry about him. Even if the whole world was ignorant of that fact, *he* knew.

I put my hands on my hips, digging my fingers into my hip bones for strength. I had to ask him a question, and I was afraid of the answer. "Con, what the hell is going on? Are you—were you *with* someone?"

I hoped the question would snap him out of this strange daze. That he'd look at me with his true eyes and say, "For fucks sake, Lily, of course I wasn't with anyone else. You know how I feel about you. It was work shit."

But instead, he lifted a shoulder. Casually. Elegantly. Cruelly. The corner of his mouth twisted down, as if he was annoyed I was asking.

My stomach flipped over. Nausea churned in it. I didn't recognize my own voice when I said weakly, "I thought you loved me."

"You did?" his eyes skimmed over my face, dispassionate. "Why?"

Why? Well because of a million things. The way he touched me. The way he looked at me. The things we had shared with each other. But the way he was looking at me now, and the way he wasn't touching me, made me realize something. I'd told *him* I loved him, but he'd never said it back. Not really.

"Because I'm an idiot," I said in that voice that didn't sound like mine. Too shrill. The syllables strangled with pain. I walked past him and jabbed at the button to summon the elevator. I thought he'd reach for me as I passed. I thought he'd said, "Oh come on, don't leave," when the door slid open.

But he did none of those things. He only turned to watch me go with mild interest. Behind him on the terrace, the candles still flickered on the table. The clouds were underlit with the hellish red glow of the city lights burning below. Against that backdrop, he looked like the devil. He looked like the pain written all over my face didn't mean anything at all.

Until the elevator door slid closed between us, I refused to let the tears come to my eyes. A hard kernel of hatred gave me the strength, but as the elevator began pulling me down away from him, it dissolved. The tears were flowing down my face in uncontrollable streams by the time the door opened on the lobby.

Even if he was the devil. Even if I *did* hate him now. I still loved him.

And I was afraid that I always would.

27

CON

After Lily left, I stood staring at the elevator while time lost all meaning. Maybe it was five minutes, maybe it was all night. All I knew was when I finally tore my eyes away, it was still night. The air had cooled, and the hellish red clouds just above were starting to scud across the sky. The smell of rain wasn't musky and fresh in LA. It carried a metallic tang. An acrid aftertaste. I breathed it in as I stepped outside. The rain was already beginning to patter lightly. The glowing flames in the candles flickered angrily as they weaved away from the tiny spats. I stood over the table for another indeterminate period of time, taking it all in. She'd gone to some trouble. I recognized the carbonara and fettuccine from Giardo's. The flowers were fresh. The candles weren't familiar. She must have bought it all before I came home, and then she'd waited here for me to return.

I couldn't picture her face. Not right now. If I had summoned the image of her face paling beneath its tan, the roses withering from her cheeks, her large blue eyes filling— I didn't know what I would do. '

I had to do it, I reminded myself. I didn't know how I was going to heal the wound the news would create in my relationship with Halley, but I knew it would be a damn sight easier if the knife wasn't still buried in the flesh. Halley might understand a fling. I'd lose her respect for a while, and it would always be between us, but we would move past it eventually. But if Lily stayed between us, I didn't know what would happen. How could she move past what stayed right in front of her?

I kept my thoughts focused on my daughter as I walked to the edge of the terrace and placed my hands, palm down, on top of the rough, chest-high wall that separated me from a thirty-story free fall. I was protecting her, the way I'd sworn to always do. The first time I'd held her, nearly twenty-two years ago, I'd looked down into her small face and swore to stand between her and pain, no matter what.

I hadn't kept it, of course. It was an impossible promise. No one could protect someone from the multitude of papercut wounds life inflicted. I'd even been the cause of the pain at times—the demands of my career pushing aside time with her. But I'd done my best. I'd learned to let go of deals when they got in the way of our vacation plans, to walk away from brutal negotiations when they threatened to overrun her high school graduation.

Now I'd learn to let go of Lily. To walk away and not look back. It was the only way.

* * *

I met Garrett and Landon for lunch the next day. I trusted all four of my friends implicitly, but I didn't need a business manager like Dominic or a producer like Julian. Right now. I needed a crisis manager and something to counteract the information Kim was about to receive.

I could tell that it killed Landon to shake his head and

spread his hands out, palms up. "I'm sorry, Con. She's clean."

I nodded grimly. I'd expected as much. After two months of being tailed, they hadn't seen Kim get so much as a parking ticket. They couldn't find anything in the last few years of her history either. And before that, it was all things the courts and Halley already knew. The cocaine arrest. The insider trading. The highly supported suspicion that she'd spent a few years working as a high-class call girl in Vegas. It was a long shot to hope that Landon had found something in the eleventh hour. But as disappointment crashed around me, I realized I *had* hoped.

Garrett leaned forward, ready to step in. "What can I do?"

I shook my head. I had no fucking clue. I'd sent clients to Garrett before when their personal lives were threatening to overshadow their professional, but I'd never needed a crisis manager myself. I'd lived the straight and narrow because I was too damn busy for detours. Besides, I didn't need him to manage the professional fallout I might experience. That would be relatively minor, unless con artists started coming out of the woodwork to claim they'd also had relationships with me and that the power differential had made them feel coerced. Those could be disproven, but the stain might remain. What I needed Garrett to manage now was how I looked to my daughter. How did I soften the blow?

Garrett was silent for a few minutes, breaking it only to order when the server came over. Finally, he looked back at me. "There are two ways to manage this with Halley," he said. "One, you put the onus on Lily. She pursued you relentlessly. Didn't want to tell her because you didn't want to ruin the friendship. Lily caught you in a weak moment. It was a one-time thing. You didn't mean for it to happen, and

194

it will never happen again. You're just as disgusted as she is."

"In other words, lying to your daughter," Landon said bluntly.

I ignored him. I was willing to lie to Halley if that was what it took. But I didn't like lying *about* Lily that way. I understood the angle, but even the idea of saying those things about her—painting her out like a gold-digging slut—made me feel sick. "What's the other way?" I asked, wincing.

Landon and Garrett glanced at each other. I had a feeling it was obvious to them, but I needed it spelled out. My usual agile mind felt like a rat in a box. It was scrambling desperately for a way out, but all it could find were walls.

"You tell her the truth before she hears it from someone else," Garrett said.

I waited for him to elaborate, but he seemed to think he'd said enough.

"This is what people pay you for?" I asked, my voice rising. "How is telling the truth managing a crisis?"

"Sometimes it's the best answer," Garrett said, unoffended. "People like the truth. It feels right when they hear it, even if they don't like it. If you want to feed the public a lie, you've got to pour enough sugar on it to disguise the taste. The truth always goes down easier."

"That's bullshit."

He shrugged. "If you say so."

I clenched my jaw, pissed he wouldn't fight back. I needed somewhere to channel all this furious, clashing energy. They let me stew until our food came. Then Garrett said, "What's wrong with the truth?"

"I can't have them both," I said immediately. "If I try to keep Lily in my life, I think I'll lose Halley."

"No one said anything about keeping Lily. I just said tell Halley the truth."

I stared at Garrett, not comprehending.

"Jesus," Landon muttered. "He doesn't even know what the truth is."

Yes, I did. I didn't want to acknowledge it, but I knew the truth. Lily had pursued me after I told her to stay away, but only because she felt the same electric energy I did. And it had never just been about sex. I'd fallen in love with her.

Garrett was laying it out for me, gently so as not to piss me off again. "What I'm suggesting is this—tell Halley the whole truth. You fell in love with her best friend. The two of you fought it because you knew it would hurt her, but it happened anyway. But even though you are in love with Lily, maybe for the first time in your life, you're willing to walk away if that's what Halley needs you to do. You really don't fucking want to, but you will."

Landon was nodding. "If you try to play this any other way, all she's going to think about is that you fucked her best friend. If you tell her *why*, it changes things. People can handle almost anything, so long as there is an explanation. A reason. A motive."

"It's the senseless acts of violence that fuck with people the most," Garrett agreed.

"Tell Halley the truth," I repeated, mulling it over. It made sense when Garrett put it like that. I could be honest with Halley about what Lily meant to me without saying, *like it or not, Lily and I are together.* If Halley genuinely couldn't deal with it, I'd stay away from Lily forever. But at least this way I had a chance of keeping my daughter and the woman I loved.

"Tell Halley the truth," Landon and Garrett agreed.

* * *

After I left lunch, I knew I didn't have much time. I didn't know when the PI was planning to hand over the information to Kim, but I knew that only seconds would elapse before Kim passed it on to Halley. I'd be shocked if she tried to blackmail me with it. Ruining me in Halley's eyes was infinitely more valuable than any pay day. She was hoping to find evidence I was hiding assets and lucked into finding out the one secret I'd kept from Halley.

Thinking about it made my back teeth clench so hard that my jaw began to ache, but I couldn't focus on getting revenge now. One day, I would. But first I had to get ahead of the story. I'd learned that much from Garrett over the years. The first person to step up usually got the benefit of the doubt. I needed every advantage I could get right now. The only thing that could make this worse would be if Halley found out from Kim instead of me.

I called her on my way back to the office.

"Hey Hals, clear your schedule. I'm taking you to dinner tonight."

"Dinner?" she said surprised. "Is this like, a Zoom dinner? You'll eat at Giardo's while I'm at Olive Garden?"

"No, we'll both be at Olive Garden, if you really want to go to that god-awful place. I'm flying in."

Another lesson from Garrett—never do important shit over the phone.

28

LILY

After I left Con's place, I wandered around LA for hours, unable to face going to Halley's condo. There were too many memories there. I'd find somewhere else to go. Anywhere. But when the rain kicked up, I admitted defeat and made my way back. I had to walk past Con's apartment building to get there, and I forced myself to look straight ahead. I wouldn't look up longingly at the pent-house, and I definitely wouldn't turn my head to stare into the lobby in hopes that he was emerging from it. I couldn't stop my ears from listening for him though. Desperately hoping to hear my name break through the quiet night. And then to hear an explanation. An apology. And I couldn't stop my mind from creating the picture of our reunion — romantic as a movie in the pouring rain.

But it never came. Instead, I just got soaking wet by walking so slowly, and I ended up in Halley's condo alone.

I couldn't leave this late at night, but I could do the next best thing. For the second time, I yanked my suitcase out from underneath the bed and threw it, open-mouthed, on the bed. Again, I began yanking my clothes from their hangers and filling it with all that I had brought and all that

I had accumulated over the last few months. I couldn't fit it all. That was fine; I didn't need it all. I began rooting through, throwing out the fancy work clothes I'd bought to impress Con. I wanted to shred the expensive lingerie, but the lace was surprisingly sturdy. I settled for throwing it in a heap on the ground with the clothes. I'd throw it all away before I left.

There was no question in my mind where I would go. Before I dropped off into an exhausted sleep, my suitcase still on the bed beside me, I booked a one-way ticket to Ohio. By this time tomorrow, I'd be back in my childhood bedroom in Yellow Springs. The one that was incongruously right off the kitchen because our house had been pieced together over multiple generations until the rooms sprawled out with no particular allegiance to a normal floorplan. My mom would be baking something in the kitchen. Hard to say what, but the sweet, yeasty smell of cinnamon rolls or banana bread would wake me up as much as the muffled thud of the oven opening and closing and the brisk metallic clink of the whisk glancing against the side of the mixing bowl.

I know I slept because when I woke up, my mouth had a thick, cottony coating and there was grit in the corners of my eyes. It had been fitful though. Haunted. I'd been searching for Con everywhere in my childhood home, convinced he was there. I kept finding new rooms. Some were filled with plants, making me think he had to be close by. I never found him though.

On the way to the airport, I thought about the actual rooms of the little Yellow Springs house. It was technically two, but my mom's room had a closet so large that it seemed like it should have been a third bedroom. It even had a window. It would easily fit a nursery. My mom wouldn't hesitate to switch rooms with me and be the one to sleep off the kitchen. She would love having me back. Dote on her grandchild.

And be completely heartbroken for me.

I called her from the terminal. She knew something was wrong just by the way I said hello. She insisted on meeting me at the Dayton International Airport even though I told her I could take a cab.

"It's a thirty-minute drive. It'll cost a fortune," she said, and wouldn't take no for an answer.

I thought I'd be ready to see her. It took me all day, with the layover in Chicago, to cross the country. I thought surely by the time the sun was coming down on what felt like the worst day of my life, I would be ready to tell my biggest supporter everything. I wasn't though. When I found her at baggage claim, I couldn't answer the questions written all over her face with anything other than a halfhearted shrug and watery smile.

The silence between us was almost painful as we waited for my suitcase, then drove the thirty minutes home. I could feel the effort it took her not to barrage me with questions. It made the air feel stiff. I wanted to spill it all, but it was like it was all bound up inside me. If I loosened the bindings, I might explode.

When we pulled into the driveway, it was dark. My mom turned off the car and turned to look at me. Her face was shadowed with concern in the sickly yellow light of the overhead. She laid her hand on my shoulder, and we sat there until the car darkened again.

"We should go in," I said, the first words I'd spoken since we left the airport. My voice cracked with disuse.

She nodded and led the way, carrying my shoulder bag while I dragged my suitcase over the paving stones that led from the driveway to the front door. Once inside, I confounded her by leaving my suitcase beside the door and walking toward her room instead of mine. She followed me into it, not saying anything when I walked to her large closet and pushed open the door. I'd been in and out of this closet my entire life. I'd made the cavernous, half-empty space my fort when I was a child. I borrowed out of it as a teenager.

I walked the length of it, stopping at the window and stretching my arms out wide. They barely brushed the sleeves of her sweaters to the left and the rough edge of her jeans hanging on the other. Plenty big enough for a small nursery.

I turned around, and nearly smiled for the first time when I saw the bemused look on my mom's face. She was trying so hard not to push me with questions, but I could tell she was dying to know what on earth I was doing, measuring her closet with the length of my stride and span of my arms.

"I'm pregnant," I said.

Her eyes widened.

I shook my head before she could ask any questions. "I don't really want to talk about...I mean, I just want to focus on the future. I want to move home and raise the baby here, at least while I'm in school. Is that okay?"

She nodded, eyes still wide, a sheen creeping across them. I could see the corners of her lips trembling with the effort of not curving into a smile. I'd expected the tears; the smile was a surprise.

"You're happy?" I asked.

She shrugged, but the smile slipped free, spreading across her face like wings. "I'm getting a grandchild," she said. Then it dimmed. "But are *you* happy?"

She could see that I wasn't, so I didn't pretend to be.

"I'm–" I turned back to the window, staring out into the darkness at the fir trees that lined the side yard. I could see the lights of our neighbor's house glinting through the foliage. I thought of standing on the sidewalk in LA, staring up at the bottom side of Con's terrace in the sky. A world away. Had I ever thought I could belong there? It seemed ludicrous now. I was a small-town Ohio girl. He was king of the city.

"You're what, honey?" my mom prompted gently, and I realized I'd never answered her question.

"I'm going to be happy," I said to the trees.

Later, she made us hot chocolate and we sat on the couch, legs pulled up beneath us, an afghan over our laps like there was a winter storm outside instead of just a sharp October chill. Telling her about the baby had been like uncorking a bottle. Now the rest of it came spilling out. She winced when she heard who the father was, but on the whole, she stayed remarkably calm.

"I'm sorry, honey," she said when I was done. "I can tell you loved him."

Love him, present tense. But I didn't correct her.

Her eyes flickered to the fireplace. The flames replicated in her eyes, reminding me of the night Con came home late to the romantic dinner I'd set up hours ago. God, had it only been twenty-four hours ago? I couldn't believe it.

"I'm so happy to have you here," she said slowly, "but I hope you don't feel trapped here, back in your childhood home. Because if he really is the head of a top tier Hollywood talent agency, you're going to have all the financial support you could ever need to raise this baby while going to school."

I'd thought of that, but the idea of it didn't give me any comfort. In some ways, it made me sick. In the end, I'd be taking money from Con after all. It didn't matter that I hadn't been after it. That I loved him. He would pay me off the way he was trying to pay off Kim.

"I know," I said dully. "I'm not worried about money. I just don't want to raise my baby alone."

Tears finally came to my eyes, instantly causing my mom's to overflow. She set her hot chocolate down on the coffee table with a thunk and wrapped her arms around me, squeezing hard. I didn't have it in me to return the hug, but I leaned heavily against her and didn't fight the embrace. I'd been running on adrenaline for the last twenty-four hours. Now I was emotionally drained and bone tired. Tomorrow I'd get up and figure out my life. Tonight, I needed to cry.

29

CON

Landon called me when I was midair, halfway to the East Coast and the inevitable. He wanted to know if I wanted him to do anything about Kim.

"Do about her?" I echoed. "Didn't you tell me you didn't have anything?"

"I told you I hadn't *found* anything," he said levelly.

I got his meaning. He always had something in his back pocket. A frame, a fix up, a trap. Did I want him to put Kim in one?

I stared at the back of the seat in front of me, considering it. It would make my life a hell of a lot easier if Landon could conjure up an incriminating counter to what Kim had on me. She'd lost the benefit of the doubt with Halley a long time ago, as much as Halley loved her. She'd know that claiming I'd framed her would only alienate Halley. It might just work...but as quickly as the temptation rose, it faded. I trusted Landon with my life, but even he couldn't guarantee that the truth would never get back to Halley. It was one thing to tell her about Lily. I could never explain blackmailing her mother.

When I told Landon not to do anything and hung up, I

felt like I was severing my last connection to my old life. The one in which I was the father I'd sworn to Halley I'd be. The one I'd spent twenty-two years building.

Strangely, as much as I was dreading telling my daughter the truth, I felt like a tether had been loosened. It was going to feel like shit to see the look on my daughter's face, but we'd come out the other side somehow. And maybe Lily would be there too.

* * *

Halley insisted on Olive Garden. That was fine with me. Better to break the news there than ruin a restaurant I liked with what was sure to be an ugly memory.

"I told you the breadsticks were amazing," she said, biting into one.

"I've had the breadsticks before, Hals." I'd ordered a beer when we sat down. I drank it now, wondering how the hell to start.

"So what are you doing here?" Halley asked when she'd swallowed. "Not that it's not nice to see you, but it's also weird, considering I'm coming home for Thanksgiving soon."

I squeezed the cold bottle tightly. Halley tilted her head at my silence. "Does it have something to do with Lily?"

My eyes jumped from the bottle to hers, shock reverberating through me. Did she know? Was she *okay* with it? She certainly didn't look pissed.

"If the job didn't work out, you can just tell me," Halley said.

I cleared my throat. "Why do you think it didn't work out?"

My daughter shrugged. Her dark curls bounced from her shoulders. "I haven't been able to get a hold of her in a few days. You showed up unexpectedly. I'm just trying to put two and two together."

"Well," I said slowly, "you're right. I'm here because of Lily. But it's not because the job didn't work out."

There wasn't a flicker of comprehension in Halley's hazel eyes. She had no fucking clue. Kim hadn't had a chance to drop the bomb in her lap yet. That meant I was going to get the full force of the detonation.

I drained my beer, throttling the neck, then set it down with a thunk.

"Dad," Halley said in surprise. "What's wrong?"

Garrett had coached me through this, but now it was all fucked up. We weren't supposed to be talking about Lily. I was supposed to tell her I'd met someone. I was happy. Then I was going to tell her everything, and end with leaving the choice in her hands.

But as I stared at the grown woman across the table, something in me unknotted. I'd done my job as a father. She was a happy, well-adjusted, intelligent adult. In a few months, she was going to shred the last layer of the cocoon I'd tried to wrap her in and pursue her acting dream. The one she kept hidden from me because she didn't want to disappoint me. The same way I'd kept Lily from her.

"Dad?" she prompted, concern shadowing her eyes. "Is everything okay?"

"I'm in love with Lily," I said abruptly.

Halley's mouth dropped open. She laughed, then she stopped short and stared at me. The color drained from her face slowly. Her eyes and her mouth formed Os. "You're *what?*"

"Neither of us meant for it to happen, but it did."

"*What* happened exactly?" Halley asked, her voice barely above a whisper.

My jaw tightened. "I told you. I fell in love with her."

"Right, but I guess I'm asking how you fell in love with her." Halley's voice rose and on the word *how* and broke at *love*. The shock and pain in her eyes sent darts of pain and guilt into my heart. I'd worked my whole life to avoid seeing that look on her face. The indisputable knowledge that I'd let her down in some fundamental way.

"Was it her personality?" Halley pressed, tart sarcasm creeping in to patch the cracks. "Her kind heart?"

"Yes," I said shortly.

Halley's laugh was hollow. "Yeah, I bet. Just like she fell in love with you for your sense of humor."

I curled my fingers around the empty beer bottle so tightly I thought it might break. I didn't want to rise to her bait, not when I saw tears gathering in her lower lashes, a silvery underline to her hostile glare. I'd never seen her look more like Kim. It disturbed me.

But just as the comparison formed, her face collapsed, and it evaporated. "God, Dad. You could have had half the women in Hollywood. You decide to fuck around with my *best friend?*"

I didn't say anything.

"And her–" Halley shook her head, her tears starting to stream down her face. She wiped them away angrily. "No wonder she hasn't been answering my calls. She's too busy being a–"

"Stop right there, Halley," I said quietly. I couldn't defend myself, but I had to defend Lily. She hadn't done anything wrong. Neither had I, for that matter. We were all adults, and it was time to fucking act like it. I'd put myself in this position by lying to my daughter, but it was time to tell her the truth.

Despite how shitty I felt, my shoulders felt lighter. I straightened them. "I'm in love with Lily, and I drove her away because I never wanted to see that look on your face."

Halley's eyes flickered in surprise. Her face didn't soften exactly, but some of the anger slackened. "What do you mean you drove her away?"

"She didn't come to work this morning. I haven't checked, but I'm guessing she's left LA."

Halley and I stared at each other across the table, the breadsticks cooling between us. "I hope you don't expect me to help you track her down," she said, her voice still cold and unforgiving.

"That's not why I came." I signaled the waiter and asked for the check.

He blinked at our empty table. "Do you want your food to go?"

"No." I handed him my credit card.

Halley watched the exchange with growing surprise. "You're just going to drop that news on me and leave?" she asked in disbelief when the waiter walked away to run the card. "Really going for that father of the year award, aren't you?"

"Hals, I'll always want to be the best father I can, but you're an adult now, and if I'd realized that sooner, I'd be better off." I kept my voice level. "I'm in love for the first time in my life, and I have to get her back."

"Even if it means losing me?" She meant to toss the words out as a challenge, but her voice broke, and her eyes filled again.

I hesitated. It was so fucking hard not to comfort her, to tell her she'd always *always* come first. But I couldn't leave my future with Lily in her hands. It was time for both of us to grow the fuck up. "I get it if you need time and don't want to see me for a while, but I'll always love you more than life and I'll always be your dad, Hals. It's just not all I am anymore."

I stood, hoping she would too. Wanting her to throw

herself into my arms like she would when she was a little girl and I was her whole world. But I wasn't anymore. And that was okay. We both had to learn to let go. When she crossed her arms mutinously–another throwback from her childhood–I nodded once and turned to go.

I had to find Lily.

30

LILY

I didn't wake up to the smell of apple turnovers or pumpkin bread like I was expecting. Instead, it was the rich, nutty smell of coffee brewing. I rolled over in bed and inhaled deeply, appreciating the scent even as I wondered about it. My mom kept coffee in the house for her best friend and neighbor, Lorraine, but the two of us preferred soda or tea. This seemed like an odd time to take up brewing it for us.

I pulled on an old, tatty robe from high school and padded out, half expecting to see Lorraine sitting at the table. Instead, I saw Con.

His back was to me, but I knew him instantly.

My mouth dropped open, and I looked from his broad shoulders to my mom's face. She smiled at me. "Good afternoon."

I stared, completely discombobulated. It couldn't be the afternoon, and that couldn't be Con.

I looked first at the clock over the stove and saw it was 12:01. I looked back at the man who had turned and stood from the table. It was really Con. Anger replaced disbelief, elbowing aside the happiness that had tried to surge at the sight of him. "What are you doing here?" I asked.

He scratched the back of his neck. "I'm getting that question a lot."

"Yeah? What's your answer?" I self-consciously tightened the belt of the robe. Why hadn't I kept the beautiful silk robe that matched my eyes? Why was I wearing something with ducks printed in irregular intervals instead? My anger took the edge on my happiness. Why was I worrying about what I was wearing when he'd treated me like dirt?

I put my hands on my hips, giving him an unobstructed view of the ducks. "Well?" I asked belligerently.

My mom quietly slipped out of the kitchen. I saw sunlight slice through the living room as she opened the front door. When she shut it behind her, I forced myself to meet Con's eyes.

"You look beautiful," he said, his gaze fastened on my face.

I doubted that. My face had to be puffy from all the crying I'd done the past thirty-six hours. "You look like you're in the wrong place," I said coldly.

"You asked what I'm doing here," Con said, shifting directions so quickly I felt disoriented again. He stepped closer. I put my hand up, palm out, warningly. "Halley asked me the same thing when I went to see her. I told her I was there to tell her about you. I told her I never wanted to hurt her, but that I'd fallen in love with you."

My mouth fell open in surprise.

"When your mom threatened to brain me with a lawn gnome if I didn't get out of her yard, I told her I wasn't leaving until I saw you, because I'm in love with you." Con took another step closer until my hand was resting against his chest.

"That's funny," I said, managing to keep an edge in my

voice even as the rest of me was dissolving, becoming bone-less with surprise and longing for it to be true. "You said something pretty different to me the other night."

Con shook his head sharply, as if trying to dislodge the memory. "I know. I was an asshole. Someone got pictures of us together, and they were going to give them to Kim. I was so fucking scared of what would happen to my relationship with Halley when she found out that I fucked over ours."

"Pictures?" I whispered.

"Yeah. She had a PI tailing me the whole time." He shook his head impatiently. "It doesn't matter. I'm glad it forced my hand. I should have never kept you a secret."

Maybe it was because I was about to become a parent myself, but I understood why he had. And even why he'd lashed out when his secret was threatened. I hadn't even met my child yet, but I knew I'd do anything for them. "I'm not asking you to choose between us," I said with difficulty. "Halley is your daughter." I couldn't tell him about the baby now. Not yet. It couldn't decide our relationship for him like Kim's pregnancy had.

Con reached for me. Pulled me closer when I didn't resist. "This isn't about her anymore. It's about you and me. I am so fucking sorry about what I said. I'll spend the rest of my life making it up to you, if you'll let me," he said into my ear.

I crumbled, unable to hold myself rigid any longer. My fingers curled into his shirt front.

His arms tightened around me "It's you and me now," he swore, his eyes blazing into mine.

"Actually," I bit my lip to hide my tentative smile, "I have a surprise for you."

I told him in a rush of words. He shook his head. "Repeat that."

"I'm pregnant," I said, slower this time. Deliberately.

212

My smile spread wider. Even if he wasn't happy about this baby, even if it changed everything between us, I couldn't hide my own joy. It was one of the only things that had kept me from sinking into total despair these hideous two days. Even if–

"We're having a baby," Con said quietly, wonderingly. The look on his face put my fears to rest. He was shocked, but he wasn't horrified. He couldn't quite believe it yet, but he *hoped* it was true.

And when the truth did finally sink in, I saw it register in his eyes. Excitement, peace, and joy. "We have to tell Halley," he said.

I winced. That hadn't been my first thought. More like, we'll have to tell Halley eventually, somehow, but God, how will we do it? "Maybe we should wait a little bit," I said hesitantly.

"No." Con shook his head firmly. "You and this baby are my family too, Lily. I want everyone to know it."

"It's going to be hard," I said, still hesitant. "Halley just found out about us, and now she'll have to deal with–"

He cut me off with a long, hard kiss. "If we've learned anything over the last few months, it's that we're lousy liars, Lily. Let's just tell the truth this time."

Joy filling me at his words, I sank into the kiss and let it wash away my own fears.

Con was right. No more secrets.

Not anymore.

CON - SIX WEEKS LATER

On December 26, Lily and I flew to Croatia. I'd told her that we could go anywhere for the week and was surprised when she picked there.

"Not the house in Aspen?" I asked.

She touched her stomach and shrugged. "Maybe next year. It's not like I can go skiing right now anyway."

"What about somewhere warm then?" I wrapped my arms around her from behind, putting my hands over hers. I imagined I could feel the beginning of a bump, even though her stomach looked as flat as ever.

"There's a heated pool. That's enough for me." She leaned her head back so that it was resting against my chest. Her golden hair smelled like the rosewater shampoo that was now a fixture in my bathroom. Our bathroom.

"Why Croatia?" I asked, trying to figure it out. The weather was cold and wet this time of year. The snow-covered castles and Plitviče Lakes National Park were something to see, but I was surprised it was her first choice.

"Because it's where it all started."

Beneath my palm, she spread her fingers out. I folded mine over them. I couldn't wait to feel my child grow inside her. "Where it all started?" I repeated. I wasn't sure what she meant. Our family had started here in LA. Probably either on the couch or the bed. Possibly in the elevator or the kitchen.

Lily angled her head back to look up at me. "That's where I was when Halley told me she'd called you, that I had an internship in LA with The Walker Agency." She laughed softly. "I was so mad at her because I was so intimidated by you."

When we got to the house on the evening of the 26th, the house manager had turned up the heat, stocked the refrigerator, and stacked fresh firewood by the fireplaces in the living room, kitchen, and main bedroom. While Lily unpacked, I lit a fire in the hearth.

"You're good at that," she observed as I coaxed the small flame to life. The stones began to glow as the fire climbed from log to log.

I straightened. "I'm good at a lot of things."

Her smile softened as her eyes heated. "It's funny," she said as I crossed the room toward her. "If you'd told me six months ago that I'd be back here with you, that we'd be—" she hesitated "—together, I'd never have believed it. Now I can't imagine anything else."

I knew why she'd hesitated. It was because, despite everything, our relationship still felt strangely undefined. She was the mother of my child. Calling her my *girlfriend* felt trivial, and I was too old to be anyone's boyfriend. Luckily, I knew what to do about it.

"I can't imagine anything else either." I brushed a lock of hair behind her ear and bent to kiss her. A long, lingering kiss, but I pulled back before her hands could lock around the back of my neck. As much as I'd like to press her down onto the bed, there was something important I had to do first.

Lily tilted her head, gazing up at me curiously. The heat was still in her eyes, her lips still gently parted. It was hard not to give her what she wanted, but there was something I wanted first. I wanted to make this official. I wanted the world to know she was mine forever, and I wanted there to be no confusion as to what we were to each other. Forget *girlfriend*, I needed Lily to be my wife.

I'd gone to Rahaminov Diamonds for the princess cut diamond ring the day after we got back from Ohio. It had been a rush order to get the diamond sourced and set in time, but the third-generation jewelers had made it happen. Now it was in a small velvet box in my back pocket. I reached for it now.

"Con," Lily protested when she saw the jewelry box. "You can't give me a present. We just had Christmas."

"I'll give you a present whenever I want," I corrected. "But this isn't a present. It's a promise."

Lily's eyes widened as she registered my words and the size of the box. Even before I opened and lowered myself onto one knee, her eyes were shining in the firelight. "Con," she breathed, one hand pressed to her lips. "I don't know what to say."

"Generally, there's one of two options," I said quietly, "but I'm only accepting one of them. Lily, will you marry me?"

She laughed and swiped at her eyes. "I hate that I'm crying. This is the happiest moment of my life. I *never* happy-cry. It must be the hormones."

"Is that a yes?"

She reached out and touched the diamond lightly with her fingers. "Yes," she breathed, but then, worriedly, "Are you sure? Halley—"

"Halley will be happy for us eventually," I said, rising to my feet. "In the meantime, you're making me the happiest man on earth. Focus on that." I pulled the ring free and slid it gently onto the fourth finger of her left hand. It fit perfectly.

Lily covered her mouth again with one hand, eyes wide as she stared at the stone. Behind her palm, I saw her smile spreading across her face even as tears dripped down her cheeks to meet the corners of her curving lips. "I love you," she said quietly, looking past the ring to meet my eyes. "And it has nothing to do with how beautiful this ring is, although it *is* beautiful. I'd marry you if you proposed with the pull tab of a tin can."

"Glad to hear it, but I don't think that'll ever be necessary." I pulled her back into my arms. "Although I am planning to take a break from the company. I feel like I missed out on too much of Halley's life. I'm not going to make the same mistake again."

"I think we'll manage," she said, melting against me. "Besides, I'm going to be a lawyer, remember?"

"Yes, you are." I kissed her, and this time when her arms slipped around my neck, I let her pull me down onto the bed. The fire jumped higher in the grate. The dark water of the Adriatic lapped at the pebbly shore. We'd traveled a long way to get here, even further than the physical distance from LA. But now we were here, and I was never going to let her go.

www.ingramcontent.com/pod-product-compliance
Lightning Source LLC
Chambersburg PA
CBHW070510160726
48003CB00004B/1513